Scottish
Bakehous:
Mysterie:

Heid and Seek

Jan Fields

AnniesFiction.com

Books in the Scottish Bakehouse Mysteries series

Library of Congress-in-Publication Data
Heid and Seek / by Jan Fields
p. cm.
I. Title
                    2021940906

AnniesFiction.com
(800) 282-6643
Scottish Bakehouse Mysteries™
Series Creator: Shari Lohner
Series Editor: Elizabeth Morrissey
Cover Illustrator: Kelley McMorris

10 11 12 13 14 | Printed in South Korea | 9 8 7 6 5 4 3 2

1

Although Loch Mallaig Elementary School had a heating system, the classroom where Carol MacCallan sat beside her husband, Harvey, felt chilly to her. She wondered for a moment if she might be coming down with something, then cut her eyes to the windows and shifted her suspicions to the delicate ice crystal patterns forming there. They reminded her of the paper snowflakes that hung from strings all around the room. Northern Michigan in January was dauntingly cold every day, and Carol missed the steady warmth of the kitchen at her bakehouse, Bread on Arrival, where she would normally be on a Friday. However, nothing would have kept Carol and Harvey from visiting the school that morning.

Harvey squirmed in his small chair, bumping his wife's arm. Carol gave him a frown.

"These chairs are not made for a man my size," he whispered.

They aren't made for a woman my size either, she refrained from saying. Instead, she shushed him and pointed her gaze to the front of the room, where a little boy with almost shockingly red hair and a face full of freckles grinned and held up his hand-drawn poster.

"My hero is my dad," the boy said. "He's an accountant, so he has to do hard math all day long." The way he said the last bit amused Carol. Clearly hard math was a terrible adversary to face.

The little boy stopped talking and waved his poster around, still grinning. The teacher's aide, Raimie Phillips, spoke up. "Kent, can you tell us what makes your father a hero?" she asked.

Kent gave her a bewildered grimace. "He does hard math all day long . . . on purpose!"

Carol chuckled under her breath. Kent obviously did not share Carol's love of mathematics, a love that had inspired her to pursue a Master's degree in the subject so many years ago and propelled her into a long career as a high school math teacher.

Carol saw the teacher's assistant struggle for a moment to suppress her own giggle.

"Yes," Raimie said. "And why does he do that?"

The little boy's face brightened. "So he can pay for all of my sister's shoes."

The adults in the room burst into laughter, and Kent tilted his head, not quite understanding why. Then, after a moment, his bright grin bloomed across his face again.

"Thank you, Kent," Raimie said, the corners of her mouth still twitching. "Now we will hear from Gavin Gilmore."

To a smattering of applause, Kent raced over to an equally freckled woman and thrust the poster into her hands before dropping into the chair beside her. The woman admired the poster, whispering to her son as he beamed at her.

Carol watched the young teacher's aide with approval. She handled the children well. Though Carol had spoken with her twin grandchildren's teacher several times at functions like this one, this was her first time seeing their classroom aide. She was certain both her daughter, Jenny, and her husband, Craig, must have spoken with the teacher's aide on many occasions, since they were both deeply involved in their children's education, and not simply because Jenny was a teacher herself. Jenny and Craig Gilmore were the kind of parents Carol had loved seeing when she was teaching, since involved parents often meant the students had strong support at home.

Carol would guess the aide's age to be early twenties. She wore a straight, beige dress and a hand-knit cardigan in natural pastels. Slender with a wide mouth, Raimie had dark-blonde hair that she wore parted on the side and pulled tightly into a ballerina bun.

Beside Carol, Harvey sat up straighter as their grandson marched to the front of the room. Carol couldn't help but smile at the child's slightly disheveled appearance. She suspected Jenny had tried extra hard to make Gavin presentable for Hero Day, but his once-neat necktie was now wildly askew and his shirt hung untucked except for a small section in the front. Still, his dark eyes danced as he reached the front and bowed deeply for the audience.

"Ham," Harvey whispered and Carol elbowed him, but not hard. She rather agreed with the assessment. Gavin did love being the center of attention.

Their grandson held up his poster and announced, "This is my grandfather, Harvey MacCallan. He used to be a newspaper reporter. Superman was a reporter too." He tapped a flapping cape on the oddly proportioned figure he'd drawn. "That's why Grandpa is wearing a cape. I don't think he wore a cape at work, but he probably should have, because that would have been awesome."

Carol cut a sideways glance at Harvey and saw he was beaming proudly.

"My grandfather got tired, so he came to live here with my grandmother," Gavin continued.

"Tired?" Raimie asked.

"*Re*tired," Harvey insisted with a bit more energy than strictly required. Carol almost laughed aloud. Far be it for anyone to see Harvey MacCallan as a tired, old man.

"Right, *re*tired," Gavin nearly shouted in triumph. But then his face crinkled in confusion. "But don't you have to be tired to be re-tired?"

Again the audience laughed while Raimie bent to whisper in Gavin's ear. His face smoothed, then he stood up extra straight and held up one finger, the classroom signal for silence. When the laughing fell away, Gavin finished his presentation. "My grandfather still writes sometimes and also makes fishing lures, but mostly he is a chicken wrangler, which is tricky because chickens are descended from dinosaurs, so they're scary sometimes."

As the applause and laughter met the end of Gavin's presentation, Carol leaned over to whisper to Harvey. "Chicken wrangler?"

Harvey shrugged. "He called and asked what my job was now. I didn't know he was going to put my answer in a report for school."

Carol patted his arm. "Serves you right for being too clever."

Gavin took two bows before Raimie gently pushed him toward his seat. He gave his grandparents a grin and trotted over to sit down beside his twin, Maisie. Behind the twins, Craig perched on another of the tiny chairs, looking every bit as uncomfortable as Harvey, and he patted Gavin's shoulder.

Maisie was sitting extra straight and her eyes shone with worry. Carol knew she loved speaking as much as Gavin once she was into it, but she suffered from more stage fright than her brother. Carol wished she sat close enough to give the girl a hug, or that Jenny hadn't had to proctor an exam for her high school chemistry students that morning.

Raimie called Maisie up to the front, and the little girl squared her shoulders and rushed toward the spot Gavin had held moments before. She stared directly at her grandmother, her eyes wide. Carol gave her what she hoped was a supportive smile. Maisie's lips quirked a bit, and she held up her poster.

The drawing was neater than her brother's, and the coloring of the figure had been done carefully. It showed a slightly lumpy person holding a cupcake in one hand and a magnifying glass in the other. For the figure's head, Maisie had pasted an actual photograph of Carol's face. The combination of drawing and photo was a little disquieting, but Carol made an effort to concentrate on the compliment of being her granddaughter's hero.

"This is my grandmother, Carol MacCallan," Maisie said, her voice much quieter than Gavin's had been.

"Please speak up so everyone can hear you, Maisie," Raimie said gently.

Maisie raised her chin and increased her volume. "This is my grandmother, Carol MacCallan. She's a superhero because she has a secret identity. Most days she is a mild-mannered baker, but sometimes she's a detective who solves *murders*." Maisie dropped her voice to a dramatic stage whisper for the last word.

Carol felt her supportive expression freeze to her face as she recovered from the shock at her granddaughter's words. She had no idea that Maisie thought she was some kind of detective.

"Even though my grandmother is a superhero, I didn't draw her in a cape because she would never wear anything that silly," Maisie said, casting a reproving frown toward her brother, who simply made a face at her. "My grandmother is more like Sherlock Holmes, only she doesn't wear the funny hat either. But she does solve lots of crimes."

Carol winced, giving up on radiating support and settling for not showing how aghast she was at this assessment.

"Is your grandma a police officer?" Kent shouted from his seat.

"No, silly," Maisie replied, equally loud now, and she shook her head as if disappointed at Kent's assumption. "She's a baker. I said that. Solving crimes is her secret identity. Police officers aren't secret."

"Inside voices," Raimie reminded them both firmly. "Do you have anything else to add, Maisie?"

The little girl shook her head, setting the beads in her hair swinging.

"Nope. My grandmother is my hero. Oh, and she's super nice too." With that, she hurried to her seat, where she and Gavin began pushing one another surreptitiously.

"Sherlock," Harvey whispered in Carol's ear.

"At least I'm not a chicken wrangler," Carol replied primly. Then she ignored him completely and focused on the remaining presentations without letting him distract her, even though he continued to fidget in his seat every so often.

As soon as the last presentation ended, a lovely young woman with huge, dark eyes stepped up to the front. It was the twins' teacher, Kendra Layville. Kendra also wore her hair pulled tightly against her head, though it formed a soft, black puff at the back instead of a ballerina bun.

Carol knew the twins adored their teacher, though they were both quite enthusiastic about all the adults at Loch Mallaig Elementary School, which Carol took as a huge commendation for the school.

"Thank you all for joining us for such a special day," Ms. Layville said, "As you've seen, the children have worked hard to honor the heroes in their lives. And I especially want to thank Raimie Phillips, my teacher's aide, for all that she's done to make this a great day for the students and their families. Now, I hope you'll all stay and join us for some refreshments."

The young woman had barely finished that last sentence before Harvey rocketed out of his uncomfortable, tiny chair. He held out a hand to Carol, which she appreciated since her seat was very low to the ground. She was rather proud of standing without a groan. The bitter cold of January did no favors for her knees.

She and Harvey headed over to congratulate the twins on their impressive reports. "I enjoyed the way you worked 'chicken wrangler' into the report," Harvey told Gavin.

"It was one of the best parts," Gavin said, and Carol almost laughed aloud at her grandson's total lack of modesty. She thought it would be nice to be so confident about everything.

"I want you to know that I'm not the least jealous that Gavin chose you instead of me as his hero," Craig informed Harvey in a somber tone.

"It's hard to compete with a grandfather," Carol said, patting Craig's arm.

"That's for sure," Craig agreed, his countenance making it clear that he admired his father-in-law nearly as much as Gavin did.

Carol felt a tug at her arm as Maisie's voice asked, "Did you see my picture?" She held up the drawing with Carol's oversize head pasted on.

Carol suppressed a grimace. "I did. And I could tell you worked hard on it. The coloring is perfect."

Maisie brightened. "I made the dress blue. Blue is beautiful."

"It is," Carol agreed.

Gavin began to tow Harvey toward the snack table, and Maisie cast a glance full of wistful yearning in that direction. "Do you want a cookie?" she asked her grandmother.

"Not right now," Carol said.

Maisie's face fell. "Are you sure? I could go get you one. We're not supposed to have any of the treats until our guests are served."

"I see. Well in that case, you'd best get one for me and one for you too."

"If you'll excuse me," Craig said. "I hate to miss a good cookie."

Maisie grabbed her dad's hand and tugged him across the room as her grandmother watched with a smile. Carol was proud of her grandchildren, and she knew the credit for their generous hearts belonged to the excellent upbringing they were getting. Jenny and Craig were doing a terrific job, and Carol was incredibly happy that her daughter had chosen her husband well.

Carol was struck with a memory of Jenny at about Maisie's age, standing before her mother with her hands on her hips and announcing she was never going to have children.

"Why is that?" Carol had asked.

"Because they're messy," Jenny said. "Every one of them. They can't help it. You should keep that in mind when you see my room."

Carol chuckled to herself. Jenny had passed that same personality along to her son.

"Mrs. MacCallan?"

Carol turned to see the young teacher's aide wringing her hands nervously. "Hello, Raimie," Carol said. "Please, call me Carol."

"Thank you. I was hoping for a chance to talk with you. I've been impressed by some of Maisie and Gavin's tales of your sleuthing."

Carol winced. "My grandchildren have rather vivid imaginations. They don't lie, mind you, but they do embellish a bit."

Raimie's expression remained serious. "Children do," she said. "But I've also read about your help with police cases in the *Crown Press News*."

"Oh my," Carol said. "That paper has an even more lurid imagination than my grandchildren. Honestly, Raimie, I wouldn't put too much stock in what they print." That was an understatement. Though Harvey insisted on subscribing to nearly all the newspapers in the region, he often mocked the *Crown Press News* for its tabloid nature and love of gossip.

The young woman's eyes filled with tears. "I was hoping you'd help us. We need it."

"What's wrong?" Carol asked, softening immediately. She had never been able to walk away from someone in need.

Raimie swallowed and dashed at her eyes. "I can't talk about it here. Could I come to the bakehouse tomorrow and speak to you privately?"

"Of course," Carol assured her. She knew her best friends and partners in the bakery, Laura Donovan and Molly Ferris, wouldn't mind if Carol took a moment to listen to the young woman's problem. They were as quick to help as Carol. It was part of what made working with them at Bread on Arrival so wonderful. They shared a love of the people of Loch Mallaig, a town they'd moved to in their fifties, which had adopted them as if they were lifelong residents.

Raimie reached out to touch her hand, relief plain on her face. "Thank you. Thank you so much."

Over Raimie's shoulder, Carol noticed a scowling man watching them from the open door of the classroom. She had never seen him in the twins' classroom before.

The man was older than Raimie, appearing to be about thirty. He wore a crisp white shirt and a navy waistcoat. Between his clothes, his well-cut dark blond hair, and his neatly trimmed beard, he struck Carol as a man who cared a great deal about his appearance.

Carol realized she hadn't heard the last thing Raimie said to her. "Hmm?"

Before Raimie could repeat herself, the man strode over and stopped beside her, whispering in her ear. Raimie paled slightly in response to whatever he said, and she stepped back from the man.

"It was nice to see you, Mrs. MacCallan," Raimie said. "I love working with your grandchildren." Then she hurried away, casting one last frown toward the man before heading to the refreshments table.

"I don't believe we've met," Carol said to the man.

"My name is Byron Quayle," he said in a reedy tenor. "My classroom is next door, and sometimes Kendra and I combine our classes for outings and such. Your grandchildren are so bright and clever." From this proximity, Carol noticed the man's pale blue eyes were a little too close together, and with his hawkish nose, he reminded Carol of a preening rooster.

"Thank you," Carol said. "We're quite proud of them."

"As well you should be," he agreed.

Though everything he said was complimentary, Carol found she wasn't warming to the man, probably because of how Raimie had reacted to him. Carol gave herself a little mental shake. *Don't jump to conclusions. He's probably perfectly nice.*

Carol knew from experience that teaching was a job best pursued by those who enjoyed the company of young people. That was part of what had motivated her in her own career before she'd retired to embark on the new adventure of owning a bakery. It was hard for her not to give the benefit of the doubt to anyone who'd chosen to make teaching their profession.

"So," Carol said, gesturing toward the refreshments table, "did you come to get a cookie?"

"Not specifically," he said, following her wave. "But now that you mention it, I think I see a chocolate chip cookie with my name on it." Without waiting for her response, he headed for the table.

On the way across the room, the teacher crossed paths with Harvey, who eyed him appraisingly. When Harvey reached Carol, he handed her a peanut butter cookie on a napkin. "Who is that guy?"

"A teacher named Mr. Quayle," Carol said. "His classroom is next door." She waved the cookie. "I thought Maisie was bringing me a cookie."

"She was petrified with indecision about which one to bring," Harvey said. "So I rescued her. Not that I expect that the particular cookie I got you could compare to the ones at Bread on Arrival."

"I'm sure it's fine." Carol took a bite and found Harvey's assessment was right. The cookie barely tasted of peanut butter and was entirely too sweet. Still, it was a cookie after all, so she took another bite.

"What did the teacher want to chat about?" Harvey asked.

"Nothing," Carol said. "In fact, I don't think he was interested in talking to me at all." In fact, she couldn't shake the impression that Byron Quayle had come into the classroom for the sole purpose of putting a stop to Raimie talking with Carol. She drew a deep breath to tell Harvey as much, but bit back the words as the twins raced over.

"The cookies are great," Gavin said. "But not as good as yours."

"That's nice of you to say," Carol replied quietly. "But maybe you should say it more quietly. Whoever made them could get hurt feelings."

Gavin cocked his head to one side. "Why? I said they were great."

"That you did," Harvey told him as he clapped a hand on his grandson's shoulder. "By the way, are you going to give me that poster you made? I'll get it framed."

Gavin's eyes went wide. "Framed like a famous painting? That would be cool."

"You can have mine," Maisie said as she beamed up at her grandmother. "In case you want to frame it too."

Carol pictured her pasted-on face watching her crookedly from a wall in her house. "That sounds lovely," she lied gently. "I'll hang it in the office at the bakery. Then Molly and Laura can enjoy it too." *And it will give me fewer nightmares.*

Maisie obviously felt that was even better than Harvey framing Gavin's picture because she made a smug face at him. Harvey quickly stepped in to be sure the twins' competitive streak didn't devolve into a squabble in the classroom.

Carol listened to them, but she was watching Raimie hand out some rather lopsided cupcakes across the room. The young woman had been truly worried about something. Carol couldn't help thinking that whatever had upset Raimie, somehow Byron had made it worse. She hoped she'd find out exactly what was going on when Raimie came to the bakery on Saturday—and that she could help.

2

Baker's hours began early every morning, so it wasn't exactly surprising that Loch Mallaig was quiet as Carol drove through town on the way to Bread on Arrival from her lakeside cabin. Still, middle January in Loch Mallaig carried a kind of crystalline silence as the night's darkness clung tenaciously despite the coming dawn. Only people with no choice ventured out before sunrise broke, bearing the illusion of warmth. Carol loved the quiet of early morning, but the cold sometimes made her feel achy and out of sorts.

She pulled into her regular spot at the bakehouse and spotted Molly Ferris and her Scottie dog, Angus, heading toward her. Angus wore an adorable plaid coat and four black booties trimmed in the same plaid. He didn't seem to be enjoying wearing the booties since his usual bouncy gate was clumpy and awkward. He lifted his tiny paws high in the air, as if trying to pull them free of the boots.

Carol swung open the door of her white Chrysler 300 and gasped at the sharp cold that met her. *How is it that I never get used to that?* She braced herself and hopped out, trying to put on a brave face to show what a hearty Michigan native she was. "Molly," she called out, proud that her voice didn't shake. "I love Angus's booties."

Molly stopped and tugged at the pale blue scarf wrapped around her neck. "Thanks. Too bad Angus hates them."

"Better to have annoying booties than frozen toes," Carol replied.

As if in response, Angus plunked down and began chewing at the bootie on his foot. Molly bent and scooped him up. "We'll be inside in a minute, and I'll take them off," she promised the grumpy dog.

Carol reached into the car, grabbed her purse and they headed inside. Even though the bakery had been closed since the previous afternoon, the air inside still carried a mix of cinnamon, fresh bread, and chocolate. Carol wondered how long it would take for the building to lose the lovely scents if it ever had a new incarnation.

The old pale-yellow Victorian that held both Bread on Arrival and Molly's cozy apartment had been through more than one total transformation over the years. Though once a private residence many years before, its first transformation had been to become Bailey's Funeral Home, which had been Loch Mallaig's largest funeral parlor for many years until the owner died in a car accident and the Victorian went on the market.

Carol, Molly, and Laura had snapped it up eagerly. Though they'd each had their own reasons for wanting a life change, the idea of opening the bakehouse together was born at a college reunion when the three former roommates came together again and reignited a dream they'd talked about so many years before. Now the dream had come true, and they all knew they'd made the best possible choice for them. Bread on Arrival was more than a business—it was home.

They'd transformed the building into a bakehouse, but kept nods to its past in their business name, Bread on Arrival, and their unique delivery vehicle, an antique LaSalle hearse. They had successfully established the bakeshop in a town proud of its Scottish heritage as the place to buy a variety of Scottish-inspired goodies, including cookies, breads, and other pastries. Their scones alone sold out nearly every morning.

Laura arrived shortly after Carol, and Molly trundled downstairs from settling Angus in her apartment. They were soon wrist-deep in bread dough, scone batter, and the normal morning bustle. While they worked, they chatted about the weather and tidbits from the newspaper. They never lacked something to discuss, though they were equally comfortable with a companionable quiet where they became lost in the work of baking.

By the time the morning batch of breads and rolls were done, the faint scents of the bakery had grown deeper and richer to fill the air and make Carol's stomach growl. "I'm going up front to grab a scone," she said. "Anyone else want one?"

"No thanks," Laura said. "I made myself a huge country breakfast this morning to fortify my body against the cold, and I suspect I will never have to eat again."

"I'll take a scone," Molly said. "My bowl of oatmeal has worn off. Get me a cranberry-and-orange scone if there are any left, okay?"

"Absolutely." Carol planned to get one of the savory scones for herself. They'd recently added a scone Molly had named "farmer's breakfast," with bacon, cheese, and chives. The thought of it made Carol's stomach growl again.

To her delight, she was able to nab the last farmer's breakfast scone and a cranberry-and-orange for Molly. More were on their way from the oven shortly, so she didn't feel guilty about cleaning them out.

Hamish Bruce, their handyman and part-time bakehouse helper, eyed the scones in her hands. "Running off with the goods again, are you?"

Carol winked at him. "Absolutely."

Hamish grumbled something after her, but she paid him no mind. She knew he simply loved to grumble and growl. None of them took him seriously anymore. When Carol had first met Hamish, she'd found him a little off-putting, but once she found out his secret—that his crusty curmudgeon act hid a tender heart—she learned to ignore his prickly moments.

Since Hamish was a fixture in Loch Mallaig, none of the bakehouse's patrons were put off by his grumbling. In fact, some of the older patrons sometimes teased him about it, then laughed at his growly replies.

Carol was nearly to the doorway leading toward the kitchen when she heard her name.

"Mrs. MacCallan?"

Raimie Phillips was crossing the room from the front door, her expression hopeful. Carol was shocked to see Byron Quayle behind her, along with Kendra Layville and a third teacher that Carol had seen around the school but didn't know.

"Let me take this scone to my friend Molly," Carol said, gesturing toward the hallway. "You can come on back to the kitchen if you want."

Raimie bobbed her head. "That would be great."

"If we must," Byron said, his tone instantly reminding Carol of Hamish, though she suspected the teacher really was as disgruntled as he sounded.

She led the group into the kitchen. She thought they could sit around the packing table and chat. January was often a slow time for their mail order business after the rush of the holidays. They tried to enjoy the momentary lull, since Valentine's Day would crank up sales for some of their more romantic treat offerings, including lavishly decorated sugar cookies and simpler heart-embossed shortbread. They even made heart-shaped strawberry scones that locals always raved about, even though Laura used frozen strawberries since fresh berries in February were about as out of season as possible.

Carol gestured toward the packing table. "We can sit here and chat. Can I get you some coffee?"

Raimie and the others all eyed Molly and Laura with open doubt. "I had hoped this would be private," Byron said.

Carol winced. She should have told Molly and Laura about the teacher's aide's request. She'd honestly forgotten. It had struck her as odd when the woman asked, but it had faded in importance in Carol's mind. Now she wouldn't blame Laura and Molly if they felt a little put upon.

"I was about to run up and check on Angus," Molly said cheerily. She grabbed her scone on the way out of the room. "Thanks so much, Carol. I'm going to eat it upstairs with a cup of tea. It'll be a nice break."

Molly breezed out of the room as if this were the best offer she'd had all day. Laura frowned at the teachers for a moment before returning to her work.

"Maybe we should hold off and do this another time," Byron said.

"No!" Raimie yelped. "Please."

Laura groaned and set down the knife she was using to chop walnuts. "Fine. We're not that busy. I could take a break." As she left the room, she cast a last glance at Carol, which was more curious than annoyed.

Relief ran through Carol. Once Laura found out what was going on, she was sure to forgive her. Of course, that meant Carol needed to learn what was going on first.

She gestured toward the chairs near the table, but as the teachers were choosing seats, she spoke to the fourth woman whose name she didn't know. "I don't believe we've met. I'm Carol MacCallan."

The woman was a few years older than Raimie, but had the same slender build. She had large dark-rimmed glasses that emphasized her small face and wore her long, brown hair loose under a pale blue knit hat. "I'm Geneva Owenby," she said. "I teach the next grade up from your grandchildren."

"It's nice to meet you," Carol said, then settled into a chair. She scanned the group, noting that three of the faces were hopeful. Only Byron's features remained guarded.

"Is there some kind of problem at the school?" Carol asked gently, her eyes on Raimie since she was the one who'd asked for the meeting.

Before Raimie could speak, Byron scoffed. "Some people think so."

The twins' teacher, Ms. Layville, quelled him by saying, "Byron, if you can't be helpful, I have no idea why you came. Let us tell Mrs. MacCallan what's been happening."

Amusement tugged at the corners of Carol's lips. She'd heard that tone from dozens of teachers and had used it herself when dealing with disruptive students in the classroom. "Call me Carol, please." After everyone responded likewise, she asked, "So what *has* been happening?"

Kendra cut her eyes toward Raimie, who nodded. "Someone has been getting into the school at night," Kendra explained. "We know because things have been taken from the teacher's cupboards."

"Things?" Carol repeated.

"Food mostly," Geneva spoke up.

Carol raised her eyebrows. "You keep food in your storage cupboards?"

Kendra chuckled. "It's not as odd as it sounds. We stock special treats for students with food allergies. No one should go without when we celebrate special occasions."

"I agree," Carol said, admiring the sentiment. She'd taught older students who didn't really have classroom parties anymore, so this was not a problem she'd ever had. She was glad these teachers were so caring. Glad, but not surprised. In Carol's experience, most teachers cared deeply about their students.

"Since the items don't have much value," Geneva said, "we didn't see it as a police matter. However, the idea of someone having easy access to the school after closing is more than a little scary. There's never been proof of a break-in beyond the missing food."

"Food that could have been snitched by a student," Byron said. "Or even the janitor. There's no reason to think the school is being broken into at all. I agree with the administration that the teachers simply need to store the stuff more carefully. I don't think your intervention is necessary."

Carol resisted the urge to glare at the rather domineering man. "I can understand why teachers are concerned about someone breaking into the school."

"But no one broke in," he insisted, punctuating his remark with a slap on the table. "And we don't need the kind of public attention this is going to draw. What happens when this leaks to the press? Parents will think their kids aren't safe at the school."

"What makes you think involving me will mean bad press?" Carol asked, struggling to keep her tone neutral.

"Haven't your past escapades ended up in the paper?" he retorted. "And hasn't that been great for business here?"

Carol blinked in shock at the clear accusation in the words.

"Please, Mrs. MacCallan," Kendra said. "Ignore Byron. We all do." She spoke right over his aggrieved huff. "He promised to behave or we wouldn't have brought him. We're sorry."

"It isn't your fault," Carol said. "But I'm not sure what you want me to do about the food."

"It isn't the food alone," Raimie said. "Someone raided the lost and found and took everything from it except for a small pair of sneakers and a three-ring binder. And those items are stored in the school office, not in a classroom."

"Doesn't prove anything," Byron muttered. "The office isn't a bunker. And kids will get up to mischief."

"Plus," Geneva said, ignoring Byron, "the kindergarten classroom lost two foam mats that the kids rest on during quiet time. The mats aren't exactly cheap, though these were badly worn and the school intended to replace them soon anyway."

"The administration has bought new locks for the kindergarten storage," Kendra said. "And they've made it plain that's all they plan to do."

"That's not enough," Geneva said urgently. "I'm scared. Someone is getting into the school at night. Some teachers arrive early or stay late when we need time for special preparation. Now I'm scared every time I have to be at the school alone."

"Are the disappearances the only indication that someone has come into the school?" Carol asked.

"The only physical one," Raimie said. "But a few days ago, I was last to leave the building because I'd been hanging up decorations for Hero Day. I heard footsteps in the hall."

"The janitor," Byron muttered, but again everyone ignored him.

"I called out. If it had been the *custodian*," she said with a sharp glance at Byron, "he would have answered. Jed would never do anything to frighten us. There was no response, but the footsteps stopped. I was scared to death." She trembled visibly at the retelling.

"I believe you," Carol said. "What do you want me to do? Should I go to the administration?"

"No," the women spoke almost in unison, obviously horrified.

"If you have to do anything," Byron said, "you must do it quietly." The other teachers murmured agreement with him.

"We were hoping you could investigate," Raimie said. "The way you've done for other people."

"I'll have to speak with Molly and Laura about this," Carol said.

The group didn't appear happy with that, but Kendra finally spoke for them. "We trust you. Do what you need to do to find out what's going on."

Byron's jaw clenched, and his mouth formed a thin, straight line of disapproval. It was obvious he didn't trust her, but he didn't offer any dissent.

"Would you be willing to start tonight?" Raimie suggested. "We're confident that the intruder will break in tonight, since it's Saturday and the building has been empty all day. The weekends would be a good time for that."

"I'll talk it over with Molly and Laura and come up with a plan," Carol promised, but she could tell they had hoped for something more decisive on the spot.

"Thank you for even considering it," Geneva said. "I hope you can find out what's happening."

"If anything is," Byron said, then stood and left the room, apparently feeling they were done. With a slightly dispirited air, Geneva and Raimie trailed after him. Only Kendra stayed behind.

"I'm sorry for Byron's attitude," Kendra said.

"That's hardly your fault," Carol said.

"I have to admit, I was almost as hard to convince as Byron," Kendra said. "Especially about involving you. Jenny will be furious if she finds out I was part of encouraging you in any kind of sleuthing."

"Jenny does worry sometimes," Carol said, mildly. "But she won't hear about your involvement from me."

Kendra thanked her, then pressed a card into Carol's hand. "This has my cell number on it. If I can do anything to help—like get you access to the building—call me. We need this solved. I'm tired of jumping at shadows once the kids leave for the day. That's not like me."

"I'll do what I can," Carol promised.

With a last thanks, Kendra left. She'd barely cleared the hallway before Molly and Laura hurried into the kitchen.

"I thought I would burst from curiosity," Molly said. "Are you going to tell us?"

"You don't have to," Laura added, though her expression was every bit as eager as Molly's.

"Of course I'll tell you." Carol related the conversation with the teachers as concisely as she could. "Despite Byron Quayle's dismissive attitude, I believe something must be going on. Teachers don't usually jump at nothing."

"Do you think one of the teachers could get us inside the building?" Laura asked.

"Kendra said she can," Carol replied, then held up the card. "She gave me her number."

Laura grinned and folded her arms over her chest, unmindful of the puff of flour that accompanied the gesture. "In that case, we need to do a stakeout and catch the intruder. Tonight."

Molly winced at Laura's mention of a stakeout. "Fergus and I have a date planned, but I could call and see what he says. Knowing Fergus, I think he'd want to be part of it."

Carol mulled that over. The teachers had been leery of word spreading, but Fergus MacGregor was as trustworthy as they come. Not only did he have deep roots in Loch Mallaig, since his family had long owned the Castleglen golf resort and lodge, but he also had the honor of dating Molly. Anyone Molly trusted couldn't help but be a winner. Carol wouldn't mind having him along for security. "You should call."

While Molly did so, Laura and Carol stood a discreet distance away, though Carol couldn't miss seeing how Molly's cheeks pinked and her eyes glowed as she talked to Fergus. She thought of the early days of dating Harvey, when a simple chat on the phone could leave her feeling happy all day.

"Are you going to invite Harvey?" Laura asked, as if she'd read her friend's mind.

"I don't plan to *invite* him," Carol said, "but I doubt I can exclude him. He can be protective in these situations." She massaged her temples.

"I wish I didn't have to tell him. Then he could profess ignorance when Jenny finds out and is mad at both of us."

"Does Jenny really worry that much?" Laura asked.

Having never had children, Laura hadn't faced the tendency for adult children to get bossy as soon as they began to notice their parents aging. *Not that Harvey and I are old by any means*, Carol asserted internally as if mentally arguing with Jenny already.

"Yoo-hoo?" Laura waved a hand at Carol. "Earth calling Carol."

"Sorry, my mind was wandering. Yes, Jenny can be a serious mother hen sometimes. I personally think she's repaying us for being strict in her teen years."

Molly joined them, still beaming. "Fergus is on for tonight."

"In that case," Laura replied, her tone suddenly all business, "do you suppose we could bake something?"

Molly and Carol promptly agreed and they all got to work, though they still discussed the details of the stakeout off and on throughout the rest of the day. By the time they closed, they had a plan, and Carol had called Kendra to arrange for her to meet them at the school at eight to let them in.

Now all Carol had to do was figure out how to tell Harvey.

3

Since she still hadn't worked out exactly how to mention the evening's plan to Harvey, Carol put off the conversation by heading to the chicken coop as soon as she got home. She told herself she was making sure the new heater was keeping her girls comfortable, but she recognized procrastination when she indulged in it.

The chicken coop was cool, but the heater kept the temperature warm enough to ensure the chickens remained healthy. Though they didn't usually lay eggs in the winter, Carol knew better than to believe that meant *never*, so she checked each nesting box. Sometimes she had to slide her hand under a rather disgruntled chicken, but she gave those hens an extra pat of apology.

Though she made sure to refresh their food and water, pet each hen, and even murmur to them a little, she soon ran out of reasons to stay outside, so she trudged to the house. *I may as well face the music.* She kicked off her shoes as soon as she came in, and padded around the house in her thick winter socks.

She always loved her home, but Carol most appreciated the log cabin in the winter. There was something about all the beams and rough timber that gave it an extra cozy warmth. Harvey had set a fire in the stone fireplace, and she paused to warm herself in front of it. She gazed out the huge windows toward the shadowy lake. Though it was still late afternoon, darkness was already creeping in, and Carol looked forward to the full moon rising later to brighten the January night.

Reluctantly, she pulled herself away from the comforting fire and went in search of Harvey. She peeked in the bedroom, which scared Pascal off the bed. The cat vanished under the bed in a gray-and-white streak.

"You can sleep on the bed during the day," she told him when he peeked out from under the dust ruffle at her. "You don't have to wait until nighttime." The extremely shy cat did sometimes cuddle up on the bed at her side, but only when he was quite sure everyone was sound asleep.

In response to Carol's chiding, the cat popped his head out of sight.

"Should have bought a dog," Carol grumbled. "Dogs are happy to see you."

Pascal didn't bother to emerge to defend himself, so Carol continued her search for Harvey. She found him slightly hunched over his laptop, completely absorbed in whatever was on the screen. *I don't want to interrupt him.* With relief, Carol put off the conversation again by going in search of a cup of tea to chase off any remaining chill from her time outside.

"I thought I saw you lurking," Harvey said from behind her a few minutes later. "Why didn't you say hello?"

Carol placed the kettle carefully on the stove. "How could you have seen me? Your back was to the door."

"A reflection in the screen," he said, then folded his arms over his chest. "You sound like you're stalling. Spill. What aren't you telling me? You didn't slide the car in the snow again, did you?"

Carol harrumphed. "Once. That happened once our first winter here, and you still act as if I'm a beginner at driving in the snow. You do remember I'm a Michigan girl, born and bred, right?"

Harvey unfolded his arms and held up his hands with a chuckle. "No need to fluff up your feathers. I'm not trying to start a fight. But I would appreciate hearing whatever it is you're avoiding telling me."

He knows me too well. "Fine. Let me get my tea, and I'll tell you all about it," she said. And she did.

Harvey's response to the plan for the evening was less than enthusiastic. "Why must you always get in the middle of these things?" he demanded.

"Says the man who spent his entire career getting into the middle of things," Carol said, then took a sip of her tea. "But I have to do something. This is the twins' school and their teachers. I can't simply ignore it."

"Fine. But I'm coming along on this stakeout." He held up one palm when Carol started to protest. "I know Fergus will be there, and I appreciate that, but it won't hurt to have both of us."

"It's becoming quite a party," Carol grumbled. "I doubt anyone would dare break in with the crowd of us there."

Harvey shrugged. "That's fine with me too."

Carol gave up. "Maybe if we're sneaky and don't all park at the school, we can manage not to turn this into a circus. I'll call everyone."

Kendra was less than thrilled to hear about another person coming along on the stakeout, but she said, "I should have seen that coming. I suppose you and Harvey are a package deal, but it would be better if we didn't tell Byron, since Harvey is a journalist."

"A retired journalist," Carol stressed.

"Mostly retired," Harvey sang out.

Kendra must have heard because she groaned. "I'll see you at eight."

After the call, Carol and Harvey made supper together, as was their habit whenever both were home at the same time. Harvey was an excellent cook, and Carol enjoyed it when he fixed her one of his specialties, like fresh fish. There was something special about cooking with him, though. The act of doing something so homey together seemed to strengthen their connection. She considered herself lucky that they still reveled in each other's company after over thirty years of marriage.

Harvey made a point of gently bumping into her now and then. "Am I in your way?" she asked, already well aware of how he'd answer.

"Not a bit," he said. "I can't help it if I enjoy being extremely close to you. It's my burden for marrying such a beautiful woman."

Carol tutted at him, but she always warmed a bit under the praise. And she was glad Harvey's mild disapproval of the evening ahead had apparently waned. They ate supper and cleaned up without a single peevish word.

Once the last dish was dried, Harvey said, "I need to finish up something on my laptop, but I'll be ready to go when you are."

"What are you working on?" she asked.

"Research," he said.

"For an article?" she asked, curious. He hadn't mentioned any upcoming projects. He still occasionally contributed to online news outlets, but he usually told her when he was doing so.

"No," he said. "This is related to fishing."

"Ah, I see. You're checking other fishing lures online again."

"You mock, but it doesn't hurt to keep tabs on the competition."

Carol chuckled as she hung her dish towel over the oven handle. "The fishing lure market is viciously competitive, eh?"

"Worse than you could imagine," he said, but his eyes twinkled, so she suspected he was teasing her.

Still, he did head off to his laptop, and Carol used the time to choose the best stakeout clothes. She assumed they'd be inside, and though the school would have cranked the heat down, it wouldn't be bitter like the cold outside. Still, she didn't want to freeze to death walking from the car, especially if they were parking some distance away for stealth. She eventually settled on several layers so she would be warm outdoors, but could shed outer garments for indoor comfort.

When the time finally came and they were driving to the school, Harvey suggested they park behind the dumpsters at the edge of the parking lot. "We'd be hidden, and we still won't have to walk far in the cold."

Carol tapped the dashboard of Harvey's Jeep Cherokee. "I don't know if even two dumpsters are enough to hide this beast."

Harvey harrumphed at the hint of criticism directed to his beloved vehicle. "We could have taken your car," he said. "But a white sedan isn't all that stealthy. If you intend to continue these clandestine operations, maybe we should trade it in for a darker color."

"Bite your tongue," she scolded. "I love my car. I expect this thing would fit, but given how perfect that dumpster idea is, someone else is sure to beat us to it."

"Worth a try."

The spot was empty when they approached, so Harvey slid the Jeep Cherokee into place behind the dumpster. It wasn't exactly hidden, but in the dark, it came close. As they crossed the shadowy parking lot, they could see someone standing under a lone light near the school's gymnasium door. At first, Carol assumed it must be Kendra, bundled against the cold, but as they got closer, she realized it was a man.

The young man was barely as tall as Carol, which is part of what made her mistake him for Kendra, though he was pale, with a smattering of freckles that stood out across his nose. He was thickly bundled, but Carol had the impression that he was slightly built. He wasn't an imposing figure, especially since he had trouble meeting their eyes as they approached.

"Good evening," he said with a bob of his head. "You must be the MacCallans."

"We are," Harvey said. "And you are?"

The man bobbed his head again. "Jed Collum. I'm the custodian. Ms. Layville said she needed me to let you in."

"Are we first?" Carol asked.

Jed shook his head. "No, ma'am. You two must be last unless you're having an awfully large shindig. Everyone else is in the gym." He opened the door and ushered them in.

Carol and Harvey both knew the way to the school's gymnasium, but they followed Jed anyway. They walked through the small foyer and down a short hall that led to the gym. Carol glanced around, noting how different the school felt with all the lights off. Only the exit lights were still lit.

"What do you think about the theory that someone is breaking in at night, Mr. Collum?" Harvey asked.

"You ought to call me Jed," he said. "I don't know what to think, honestly. I'm careful to lock up every day, so I don't know how anyone could get in. But I feel bad about the teachers being scared."

"That's understandable," Carol said.

They walked into the gym, where one bank of lights was on, illuminating Kendra and their friends in a small group. They all hurried over to greet Carol and Harvey. "I thought the chickens might be holding you up," Laura said.

"Nope," Carol said. "Harvey is simply an extremely careful driver at night when it's snowy."

"She means 'slow,'" Harvey said. "But I have precious cargo, and I won't apologize for being careful."

Carol rolled her eyes and apologized for keeping them waiting. "It was nice to meet you, Jed," she said. "I thought you'd probably be the one to let us in, Kendra."

"No, ma'am," Jed said from behind them. "I am responsible for these." He shook a large ring of keys, making them jangle. "I don't hand them over to anyone."

"But Jed is always willing to let any of us in and out when we have to come in early or leave late," Kendra said. "He's a gem."

Jed bobbed his head, then muttered something about heading to his office.

"You have an office?" Harvey asked.

Jed cleared his throat and shifted nervously. "Kind of. It's the furnace room in the basement with a few furnishings added, but it's the closest thing I have to an office." Then his intense eyes zeroed in on Kendra. "You let me know when you're ready to leave. I'll let everyone out."

"Of course, Jed," Kendra said. "Thank you."

As the custodian shuffled away, Carol watched him. He had sounded concerned about the teacher's fears, but he was the one with the best opportunity to be the thief. He could come and go whenever he wanted. She wondered how much the school custodian was paid. Was it possible he felt he needed the food even more than the teachers or the children? Could he be the one causing the problems?

4

"I thought we would split up into groups," Kendra said, interrupting Carol's thoughts about Jed Collum. The teacher stood straight and tall, very much in command of the situation. Again, Carol was struck by how familiar the stance was. More and more, Kendra reminded her of a younger version of herself.

"Doesn't the gang always get into trouble when they split up?" Fergus asked, his tone playful.

Kendra blinked at him. "The gang?"

Molly gave Fergus a wry side glance. "He means on *Scooby Doo*. Fergus loved that show when we were kids. You don't know how many times I got to hear 'ruh-roh!' when I was visiting Loch Mallaig in the summers."

"From the TV or from Fergus?" Laura asked.

"Both," Molly answered.

Kendra's expression was strained. "I still think it would be wise to split up. We can take up different positions around the school and listen for any movement."

"Sounds good to me," Molly said, then pointed at Fergus. "But no dog voice. You can be Shaggy for a change."

"No, he cannot," Harvey insisted. "Because if he's Shaggy, then as the only other male in this group, I'm Scooby, and I refuse to speak dog."

"Ruh-roh," Fergus said.

Laura tapped her foot impatiently on the wooden gym floor, the sound reverberating in the still air. "Maybe we could concentrate on the stakeout."

Carol agreed firmly. She didn't want to rain on anyone's fun, but she'd seen how afraid Raimie had been when she described being at the school alone with the creepy footsteps. She thought they owed it to the young woman to find an answer so she could work without fear again.

"Scooby and I will check the area around the office where the lost and found was ransacked," Molly suggested.

"Sounds good." Laura turned to Kendra. "How about you and I take one of the wings?"

"We can take the upper wing," Kendra agreed. "Carol, can you and your husband take the lower wing? The one with the art room?"

"We can," Carol said. "Holler if anyone finds anything."

Fergus and Molly left first, and from the way Fergus nudged Molly slightly on the way out the door, Carol doubted it would be long before he'd be holding her hand in the dark hallways. She was glad Fergus and Molly were dating. They were good for each other, much the way she and Harvey were.

Kendra waved for Harvey and Carol to leave the gym second. Carol suspected she was going to switch out the lights behind them to hide their presence in the school. As she passed Laura, Carol's musings about Molly and Fergus switched to Laura's personal life. Laura had insisted she was supremely happy being single for years. She was presently dating Trent McKade, who owned Northern Woods Outfitters, and Carol had high hopes for that relationship though she knew better than to mention it. Carol admired Laura's independence, but hoped her dear friend would someday enjoy the kind of happiness she and Molly had in their lives. At least Trent was at a business convention, so they hadn't had to include him in their unduly large group at the school—not that Carol would have minded for Laura's sake.

Harvey took Carol's hand and gave it a tug. Carol realized she'd slowed as she was pondering love lives. Her cheeks warmed at having given into woolgathering when they should be focused on the task at hand. She strode purposely out of the gym as if to make up for her earlier dawdling.

She and Harvey headed down a dark hallway toward the lower wing of the elementary school. During the day, the hall would be bright with all the projects taped to the walls and the cheery bulletin boards bearing inspiring messages about sharing and responsibility. In the dark, those bulletin boards were little more than slightly darker blotches on the walls, and chairs along the wall became squatting shadow figures. It was all kinds of creepy.

"We should find a good hiding spot," Carol said when they'd reached their assigned wing without incident. "We can wait and listen." She scanned the line of doors on either side of the hall. She supposed any of the classrooms would do.

"How about the art room?" Harvey suggested, and they stepped into the room. Harvey carefully closed the door to a bare crack and they stood beside it, attentive to the quiet.

"Remember, we have to be quiet," Harvey whispered. "No shouting."

"Of course we have to be quiet," she said, puzzled by his remark. By the low light of a lamp the art teacher had left lit on her desk behind them, she noticed Harvey had a mischievous gleam in his eye. "What are you up to?"

"I simply thought this was a perfect time to tell you something," he said, feigning innocence. "Last week, I got a call from some of the other retired codgers I used to work with and they invited me on a fishing trip to the South Carolina coast. I thought about it for a while and researched places to stay, and I'd like to go."

"All right," Carol said, still not sure why he sounded so tentative and unsure. After all, he'd gone on fishing trips before. They loved their time together, but she and Harvey had never felt it necessary to be joined at the hip.

"Well, two of the guys are bringing their wives. One of them is Paul Harris. You met his wife, Betsy, a couple times when we worked together."

Carol agreed quietly. She remembered Betsy as an energetic woman with a lively sense of humor. She'd enjoyed talking with her. Still, she wasn't sure what Harvey was trying to say. It wasn't like him to be so roundabout. "Harvey, what are you trying to say?"

"I was hoping you would want to come," he blurted. "You wouldn't have to fish. When I was researching, I saw there were a lot of interesting places in the area, and I even saw a crafting expo listed."

Carol chuckled at how hard Harvey was trying to sell the idea of a trip. She wouldn't mind a weekend away. Of course, it would mean airfare, which was no small expense, but they didn't splurge that often. "It sounds nice. Why do I sense there's a catch?"

"The trip will last a week, maybe a little more with travel time," he said. After a final hesitation, he added, "And they want to go in about two weeks."

"From now?" Carol gaped at him. "I can't possibly up and leave for a week on such short notice. You know I have a business to run." When he opened his mouth, she held up a hand, anticipating what he was going to say. "Co-run. Still, I take my responsibilities seriously. I handle all the books for the business, and I do a fair amount of the baking. I can't justify deserting Laura and Molly for a week." Carol realized her voice was creeping up in volume, so she stopped speaking and took a calming breath. She knew Harvey did take her work seriously. She didn't need to let it upset her.

Instead of backing down, Harvey met her eyes for a long moment and said, "I've heard you say multiple times that business slows down this time of year. So what time could be better? This move to Loch Mallaig was supposed to help us spend more time together."

"That's not fair," she whispered fiercely. "We spend a lot of time together. We cook together. We take care of the chickens. We even get to go to the twins' school functions."

Harvey gestured toward the barely cracked door. "A case in point."

Carol was still a little upset. "I love spending time with you, but a weeklong trip on short notice is a lot to process."

"Please promise you'll think about it," he said. "And talk to Laura and Molly about it. I bet you'll find them completely on board with the idea."

"You've already talked to them about it, haven't you?" Carol asked.

"Not a word," he assured her. "But I know how much they care about you. They'll want to see you go and have fun."

Before Carol could answer that, they heard shouting coming from somewhere in the school. "That's Fergus!" Carol cried.

Together they dashed out in the hall, cutting the corner into the hallway so tightly that Harvey nearly tripped over one of the small chairs leaning against the wall. Carol caught his arm to help him get his balance, then they raced up the hallway. They froze when Fergus shouted again from somewhere out of sight.

"Someone is in the building!" Fergus yelled. "He's heading for you!"

"Does he mean us?" Harvey asked, stepping protectively ahead of Carol. "Maybe you should wait in the art room."

"I don't think so," Carol said, using her firmest teacher voice. She peered around him into the darkness. "I'm not leaving you here alone. Should we search for the intruder or wait for him to come to us?"

"I'm not going to look for trouble with you here," Harvey said, his voice as unyielding as Carol's had been. She knew he wasn't going to be moved on that, so she squinted into the darkness ahead.

They heard the sound of many feet thundering down the hall. If the intruder was heading toward them, he was being pursued. Did that make it foolish to stand and wait for him? What if he was desperate? Or armed? She braced herself and could tell by the stiffening of his back that Harvey was doing the same.

The sound of footsteps grew nearer, then they spotted a group wheeling around the far corner and heading toward them. Carol released a pent-up breath when she recognized them easily as Fergus, Molly, Kendra, and Laura.

"He was ahead of us," Fergus said once they had met up. He and the others panted with their efforts. "Where did he go?"

"He never came around the corner," Harvey said. "We would have seen him. And before we came out of the art room, we would have heard him. No one came down this hall."

Kendra caught her breath enough to ask the question on everyone's mind. "In that case, where is he?"

And to that question, not a single one of them had an answer. They decided to backtrack as a group and search every room in the school. They passed through the halls together, moving slowly and splitting up only to search rooms on opposite sides of the hall as they reached them. Though a few of the rooms were locked, most of the doors opened, and they were able to see the rooms were empty. They were careful to check behind, under, and even inside furniture whenever it offered a potential hiding spot.

At last, they stopped in front of the main office. "The intruder must have gotten past us somehow," Laura said, frustration clear in her voice. She pulled an elastic from her jeans pocket and pulled her hair into a ponytail, her jerky movements another sign of irritation.

"I don't know how he could have," Fergus said. "There's no door to the outside anywhere in the upper wing, is there, Kendra?"

She shook her head, her dark eyes reflecting as much frustration as anyone else. "I know it's impossible, but he seems to have vanished."

Molly gestured to the acoustical tile on the ceiling. "I've seen movies where people crawled up into ceilings."

"That doesn't happen outside of movies," Harvey said. "The framework that holds those tiles in place couldn't take the weight of a person. Ceiling tiles are light, so you don't need anything strong to hold them up."

Molly shrugged. "Well, he must have gone somewhere."

Then Carol had an idea. "If the intruder couldn't get out and couldn't go up, how about down? Where is the door to the basement?"

Kendra blinked. "It's toward the upper wing. But if someone ran downstairs, Jed would have heard. We'd know by now."

"Unless he hurt Jed," Carol said, her voice soft as she hated to even entertain the idea. But her tone couldn't make the possibility any less dreadful, and Kendra's dark eyes widened.

"Jed!" Kendra dashed down the hall with the rest of them right behind her.

Kendra wrenched open a door and hurried down the stairs, calling the custodian's name as she descended. Carol heard a bang and then shuffling. Jed appeared at the bottom of the stairs and Kendra nearly plowed into him.

"Are you all right, Ms. Layville?" he asked.

"Oh, Jed, there you are," Kendra said. "I thought you might be hurt."

"I'm fine," he said, staring at her in perplexity.

Fergus edged around Kendra. "Jed, did anyone come down here between the time you left us in the gym and right now?"

Jed shook his head. "No, sir. Though I nodded off a bit. It's warm and cozy next to the furnace, and I have a nice chair."

"So someone could have come down and you wouldn't have known?" Carol asked.

He shook his head. "Those stairs are creaky, ma'am. I would have heard. I'm a light sleeper."

Maybe. Carol surveyed the shadowy basement. "We should still go over everything. Is there outdoor access from the basement?"

Jed rubbed the beard stubble on his cheek. "Of course. It's in the fire code."

"Can you show us where that is?" Carol asked, feeling as if she were dragging the young man along. Judging from how slowly he was processing the discussion, she suspected he was a much heavier sleeper than he claimed.

Jed led them to the door. "It's locked on the outside," he explained. "But you can release it from in here in case of fire."

"It says the alarm will sound," Harvey said, reading from a sticker on the release latch.

Jed raised his shoulders in a sheepish shrug. "The alarm doesn't work. I told Mrs. Dour it ought to be fixed, but she says money goes to students, not silly buzzers."

Carol assumed he meant Camilla Dour, the principal of the school. It sounded like her. Carol had only met the woman a few times, but she gave the impression of being completely committed to the students. Still, door alarms were there for a purpose, and safety was important for the students too.

Harvey pushed open the door, and the group huddled around to examine the scene outside. The door had cut through a pile of snow, but Carol couldn't tell when that had happened. She wished she'd been the one to open the door because the amount of resistance she met would have been information. Beyond the arc of pushed-aside snow, they could see deep imprints. Someone had come out this door—but when?

"It appears we have the answer to our disappearing intruder," Harvey said.

"I don't think so," Jed insisted. "Those tracks probably aren't fresh. It hasn't snowed in a couple days, and the kids sometimes play a game where they run up to the door, smack it, and run away. They think there's a monster down here."

"Why would they think that?" Kendra asked.

"The furnace makes noises sometimes," Jed said, dropping his voice to a guilty mumble. "Reminds me of a monster, so I probably said something about it to a couple of the kids."

Kendra rolled her eyes but didn't scold the man.

"I still think this door is the most likely exit for our intruder," Harvey insisted, and Laura quickly piped up in agreement. Carol agreed, but didn't voice it. She could see Jed was already feeling defensive about the possibility that he'd slept through the intruder coming downstairs.

Fergus examined the door. "I wonder if it could be the entrance for the intruder as well."

"No," Jed said. "It's locked to anyone trying to open it from the outside."

"Maybe we should check," Fergus said. "I'll go out and try it. Open up when I bang on the door so I don't freeze to death."

"It won't let you in," Jed said stubbornly. "The door locks. I'm not wrong about *that*."

"Doesn't hurt to make sure." Fergus pushed the door open again and stepped out. The door swung slowly closed. They heard the sound of someone trying to pull the door. It rattled slightly, but did not come open. Seconds later, a rap sounded, and Harvey let Fergus in.

"I told you," Jed said.

"And you were right," Fergus agreed cheerily. "Which means we still don't know how the intruder got in."

"Maybe we should try all the doors," Kendra said gently. "To make sure the locks work."

"They work," Jed grumbled, but he led the group upstairs, and they walked through the school again. Each time they came to a door, a different member of the group would go outside and try to get in so that Fergus didn't have to freeze in the icy night air over and over. They discovered that Jed was correct. All of the doors had been locked tight.

"Do you suppose the person could have gained access through a window?" Laura asked.

Kendra shook her head. "Most of the windows don't open far even if they are unlocked, which they shouldn't be this time of year. We don't want kids sneaking out the windows when their teacher steps out for a minute."

"Isn't that a fire hazard?" Laura asked.

"No," Kendra said. "The mechanism that blocks the window opening can be disengaged, but you have to know how. I don't think anyone is coming in the windows. Besides, we all have space and storage issues in the classrooms. None of the windows are particularly easy to access. If someone crawled in one, the person would knock over all kinds of stuff."

"There's one other possibility," Carol suggested. "What if the intruder got in Friday when school was in session and stayed here? If the person had a good hiding spot and those mats for sleeping, it wouldn't be a bad place to get out of the cold."

"No," Jed said, and this time he sounded a little angry. "I do my job. I don't leave people in here for days and not notice. And the doors are locked while school is in session, so someone would have had to let them in. I know you're all trying to do the right thing and imagine what could be happening, but don't imagine that I'm not doing my job."

Kendra held up a placating hand and spoke gently. "Everyone knows you do a great job, Jed. I wouldn't suggest otherwise."

Jed's features grew less defensive, but he didn't say anything else. With no fresh ideas, the group stood in the hall and stared at one another.

Then they all jumped at the sound of hard banging coming from the main entrance to the school. They sprinted toward the sound.

Jed hauled the door open, and Carol saw Camilla Dour standing out on the covered walkway in front of the school. She was wearing a smart black wool coat and matching muffler. The short, silver hair Carol remembered from previous encounters was covered by a snow-white knit cap. The hat softened the otherwise harsh angles of the principal's appearance, but did nothing for her furious expression.

She stormed into the building with Byron Quayle in tow. Carol hadn't even spotted him when she'd first seen the principal. Who'd notice him next to the principal's commanding presence?

"What are all of you doing here?" the principal demanded.

"Since you have Byron with you," Kendra said, "I assume you know the answer to that."

Camilla glowered at Kendra. "So you are here chasing Raimie's ghost."

"Raimie never said she saw a ghost," Kendra said. "She saw an intruder, and that's exactly what we saw here tonight."

Camilla raised her eyebrows. "We? You all saw an intruder here?"

"No," Molly said. "Only Fergus and I saw the intruder. We were coming out of the office, and we saw someone standing in the hall. We gave chase and the person vanished, but we know now that he probably went downstairs."

"Maybe," Jed cut in. "Maybe went downstairs. But probably not."

The principal had visibly bristled when Molly said she and Fergus had been in the office, then she'd cut her eyes toward Jed as he spoke.

Now she peered at Molly. "Can you describe this intruder?"

"The person was thickly bundled against the cold," Fergus said in a transparent attempt to pull the woman's ire away from Molly. It worked, as Camilla glared at him instead. "Also, he ran as soon as he spotted us, so we had no chance to identify him."

"But you're sure this wasn't simply a figment of your imagination?" the principal asked in a tone that made it clear she thought the sighting was exactly that.

"It was no figment," Molly said.

"Nor were the footprints we found in the snow outside the basement door," Harvey said.

"I explained to them that the kids run to the door down there sometimes, and it tears up the snow," Jed added. "They can't get in, but it's a game."

"Whoever the intruder was, we were trying to help," Carol said. "This is my grandchildren's school, and we want to be absolutely certain that it's safe for the children and their teachers."

The principal shifted her attention to Carol, who lifted her chin and met Camilla's gaze. She'd dealt with administrative bullies in her life, and she knew that it never paid to give in to them.

Finally the principal's demeanor softened a fraction. "I understand your concern for the children," she said. "And I share it. Nothing will be allowed at Loch Mallaig Elementary that endangers a child in any way. I assure you that nothing is happening, though I promise we will consider Raimie's concerns and the concerns of any other teachers." She shot a quick glance at Kendra. "Now, I don't think there is anything else you can do tonight. Would you please go home so we can lock up?"

Carol didn't want to leave with nothing resolved, but she was certain the intruder was gone and that they'd done all they could, so she acquiesced. They began to file out the front door, but Camilla stopped Kendra. "Ms. Layville, may I have a brief word?"

Carol gave Kendra a supportive smile, but the principal practically closed the school's heavy door in her face. She suspected Kendra's next few minutes were going to be anything but pleasant.

"I hate to leave Kendra in there," Carol said to Harvey.

"Nothing we can do," Harvey said, but he put a comforting arm around Carol. "Besides, she reminds me of you. I'm sure she'll be fine." The comment forced a small chuckle from Carol, as she'd been thinking the exact same thing earlier.

Disheartened, the group trudged through the front lot. "We're parked over behind the dumpster," Carol said.

"We're that way too, over in the next driveway," Fergus said. "The house at the end of the drive there is completely empty, so we didn't think anyone would mind."

"I'm there too," Laura said. "I followed Fergus and Molly."

As they drew closer to the dumpster, Harvey grabbed Carol's arm. "Hey, the lid is open. It wasn't when we parked."

"I can vouch for that," Laura replied. "I saw it when we walked by on the way to the school."

They stood stock still and listened for the sound of someone hiding in the dumpster, but the cold night was completely silent. Finally, they slowly approached the dumpster, walking close together.

Then Molly yelped. "A shoe. That wasn't there before." She indicated where a shoe lay partially wedged into the space where the bottom of the dumpster almost met the pavement.

"Maybe it's one of the shoes from the lost and found," Laura suggested as they crept forward, all nervous about what they might find.

"I don't think so," Carol said in a choked voice. She and Harvey had somehow ended up at the front of the group as they'd approached, so she got the first clear view of the shoe. It wasn't empty. It was on the foot of a person who lay unmoving on the snowy pavement behind the dumpster. A whimper escaped Carol's mouth before she could stop it. No one would nap in the snow on an icy winter night.

They'd found a body.

5

Before anyone else could even move from the shock, Laura whipped out her phone to call 911. Fergus knelt beside the bundled body on the pavement and managed to push one sleeve high enough to feel for a pulse on the pale wrist. Carol still couldn't guess whether the person lying so still on the ground was a man or a woman.

"Did you find a pulse?" Molly asked, her voice pitched higher than usual from the stress of the situation.

Fergus shook his head. "No. And the skin is cold."

"Can you try the carotid?" Harvey suggested. "In this weather, I'm not sure cold skin is proof enough."

Fergus had to dislodge the thick scarf wrapped around the person's face to reach the carotid artery. As the heavy, knitted scarf was pushed aside, Carol caught her first sight of the victim's face. It was gray in the shadowy night and deeply wrinkled.

"Definitely no pulse," Fergus said finally, then shifted his position to begin CPR, which was no easy task with the layers and layers of clothing. The clothes were a hodgepodge of colors. Even the mittens on the person's hands were mismatched.

"Poor soul," Carol whispered as Fergus worked.

"From the clothes, I suspect it's someone homeless," Harvey said.

Laura finished her call and slid the phone into her coat pocket. "Help is on the way. I hate to think of homeless people in Loch Mallaig. It makes me feel that we're failing somehow as a community."

"I know what you mean," Harvey agreed. "But homelessness is complicated. I wrote several pieces about it when we lived in Pittsburgh, and the reasons behind homelessness are as complicated as the people involved, and as hard to solve."

Laura murmured some vague agreement, but Carol could see the reluctance in her friend's eyes. Carol felt it too. As a community, they should have been able to prevent this somehow.

Sirens sounded in the distance, then grew ever closer. Soon the parking lot was full of flashing lights. Carol watched the school, expecting the principal to come out in response to the sirens, but she didn't see anyone, not even Kendra and Jed.

Emergency workers took over for Fergus, who moved aside with palpable relief. Carol felt the same, as if having trained professionals there made everything a little better. Still, despite the speed and professionalism of the workers, the person on the ground never woke up.

"Fancy meeting the lot of you here," Officer Michael Drummond said drily. "I'm beginning to think Loch Mallaig can't have an emergency without at least one of you."

"And now we've had one with all of us," Harvey replied.

The officer gestured toward the victim, mostly shielded by the emergency workers. "Anyone you know?"

The group shook their heads. "Though it's hard to tell," Fergus said. "I could barely reach skin to check for a pulse, and I couldn't begin to guess if that's a man or a woman."

Officer Drummond rubbed the bridge of his nose. "I imagine we'll know at least that much soon enough." He pulled a pad and pen from the pocket of the heavy jacket he wore. "So, what are you folks doing at the school on a Saturday night? Was there a school function?"

The group exchanged glances. Kendra and the teachers had been hesitant about their concerns getting out, but now someone had died.

Surely they owed the police the truth. Finally, all eyes settled on Carol, clearly intending for her to make the decision.

"We came to investigate a concern some of the teachers here have had," Carol said. "They thought someone might be getting into the school after hours. A few things have gone missing, and one teacher's aide thought she heard someone in the halls when no one should have been there."

The officer raised an eyebrow. "And did anyone call the police?"

"Apparently the administration preferred they not do that," Carol said. "Instead, the teachers asked if we'd help."

"Being Loch Mallaig's answer to Miss Marple, times three," Officer Drummond said. Then he gestured at Harvey and Fergus with his pen. "And cohorts."

Laura scoffed. "I don't think we're old enough for a comparison to Miss Marple."

The officer grinned. "Then the Nancy Drew gang. How's that?"

"Before you worry about naming them," Fergus said. "You should know that we did spot someone in the school. The person was heavily bundled against the cold. Unfortunately, they got away before we could ask any questions."

Officer Drummond indicated the victim. "Do you think that's the person?"

"I don't know," Fergus admitted. "Molly and I caught only a brief peek. Maybe? But I have to say that it sounds a bit unlikely to me. The victim's skin was ice-cold, even under that heavy scarf, so I'm certain the coroner will find he or she has been there for a while."

"Not too long, since no one was there when we parked," Harvey said. "We would have noticed, especially because we were searching for you guys in the parking lot."

"It's dark," the officer said. "Maybe you missed him or her."

"They're lying within a foot or two of the front end of my car," Harvey said. "I believe I would have noticed."

The officer wrote down everything without further comment. Carol's gaze kept drifting to the knot of people around the prone figure. One of the emergency workers stood up and stepped away from the victim to approach them. Carol realized she was holding her breath, tensing against what this man had to say.

The man raised a hand toward the officer. "Mike," he said.

"Anything you can tell me, Ballard?" Officer Drummond asked.

The man withdrew heavy gloves from the pocket of his coat and pulled them on as he spoke. "Not much. We had to loosen more clothes to work, so I can tell you that it's a woman. My guess would be that she was in her upper sixties, though if she's been living rough, that can make a person appear older than they actually are."

"Froze to death?" the officer asked.

Ballard shrugged. "I'm no forensic scientist, but when we pulled her hat off, we found a fair bit of blood. Something smacked her in the head, hard. I don't know if it killed her, or if it knocked her out and the cold finished the job. The coroner should be able to tell you." He pointed at the all-metal dumpster. "I'm thinking it could have been the lid of the dumpster. Those lids are heavier than people think. If she was trying to open the lid and it slipped from her grasp, it could have slammed back and struck her."

Ballard headed toward the rest of the emergency workers, who were packing up their gear. Carol saw Fergus step away from Molly and head after the man, stopping him for a moment. She couldn't hear the brief conversation, but it couldn't have been more than a sentence or two.

Carol considered the dumpster and the area around it. She pondered the position of the body. If the victim had been reaching into the dumpster and it hit her, why was she behind the bin instead of in front of it? Had she been conscious enough after the blow to walk to the rear of the dumpster? But that didn't make sense. The dumpster was open, not closed. So if the woman had been struck by the lid, she must have been behind the dumpster and it struck her when someone else flung it open too far. In that case, the victim couldn't have been the one who opened the dumpster. There must have been more than one person.

And who was that other person, that hadn't stopped to make sure this poor woman was okay?

Carol watched Officer Drummond, wondering if she should voice her theory. They still didn't know that the blow had been from the dumpster lid at all. If it was, she knew from experience that Michael Drummond was more than smart enough to figure out what Carol had.

She was still debating whether to speak up or not when they heard a familiar voice roaring across the parking lot. "What are you people doing out here?" Camilla Dour was storming toward them. "I told you to leave."

"Let's stay calm," Officer Drummond said as the principal reached the group. "Mrs. MacCallan and the others found a body near the dumpster, and they stayed to render aid and to answer my questions."

Mrs. Dour's fierce anger fell away at once, and the color drained from her cheeks. "A body? What are you talking about?"

"I'm talking about a death. I assume you don't know anything about it?"

The principal's previous demeanor returned at once. "Me? Of course not."

"Have you had problems with anyone going through the contents of the dumpster?" the officer asked.

"Not as far as I know," she said. "Though if there was no mess, I probably wouldn't know about it."

Officer Drummond appraised her. "But you were aware that someone had broken into the school?"

The principal glared at Carol and the others again. "That is a ridiculous story that one of our young teacher's assistants started. I have no idea why anyone involved this lot."

Harvey actually laughed aloud at her reference to them as *this lot*. Carol gave him an approving smile. She was proud of him for resisting the woman's efforts to be intimidating.

Carol opened her mouth to make a retort, but the principal launched into a new line of complaint.

"I hope you will keep the location of this unfortunate person's death out of the press," she said firmly to the police officer. "The community does not need to begin thinking their children aren't safe."

"Are you certain they are?" Carol asked.

The principal's face reddened still further, and her next words came out as all but a snarl. "Of course they are safe here."

Carol didn't bother arguing with the irate woman, but she did wonder if it could be a good time for the twins to take a little break. As bright as the children were, it wouldn't be difficult for them to catch up if they took a few days off. She made a mental note to discuss it with Jenny.

"All right," Officer Drummond said. "You are all free to go since I've spoken with you already, unless you can think of anything else you need to tell me."

"No, nothing," Carol said, and the others echoed her sentiment.

"Then you'll get a call sometime on Monday to come and sign an official statement," the officer said. "But if you think of anything before then, don't hesitate to call."

"I shall be on my way as well," the principal said.

"Actually," Officer Drummond said, and Carol detected a hint of amusement in his voice. She suspected he rather enjoyed thwarting the principal's authority. "I do have a few questions."

Camilla crossed her arms over her chest. "If you must."

Harvey began to herd Carol toward the car, and the others walked along beside them. "I hate to go before I see the poor woman's face clearly," Carol said. "We get so many people in the bakehouse. One of us might recognize her."

"I'm sure the police will identify her soon enough," Harvey said. "And it's not going to help anyone if we all end up with frostbite."

With a shiver, Carol had to admit she was cold, especially now that the adrenaline rush of the emergency had ebbed. "Fine," she said, making an effort not to let her teeth chatter.

At the Jeep, Laura, Molly, and Fergus bid them all good night before hurrying along to their own cars. Carol didn't doubt they were chilled through as well. Harvey opened the car door for her and she climbed inside, trying to ignore how cold the interior was. *At least I'm out of the wind*, she told herself, wrapping her arms tightly around her chest.

Harvey cranked the car and the heater blew cold air at Carol, disproving her belief that she couldn't feel any chillier. While she shivered, she peered at the school and spotted Kendra and Jed standing near the door that they'd entered a few short hours earlier. Kendra's expression was horror-stricken, her gaze fixed on the men strapping the body onto a stretcher for transport.

Still, it was Jed who caught Carol's eye. He stood with his arms hanging loosely at his side and his face slack with shock. He was white as a sheet.

Of course the situation was upsetting, but this seemed to be more than that. Why would the school custodian be so affected by the appearance of a body?

6

After church the next morning, Maisie and Gavin scrambled quickly out of the car and raced ahead of Carol and Harvey toward the MacCallans' house.

"Watch for ice," Carol called out, knowing full well the twins wouldn't do that. They were full speed ahead all the time.

Sure enough, the two actually picked up speed as they raced along the walk.

"Don't worry," Harvey said. "At their age, they bounce."

"I'm not sure that's scientifically correct," Carol replied.

The twins had reached the door and were loudly squabbling about which of them had gotten there first, who'd touched the doorstep first, and who'd touched the door first.

"While I'm laying out the food," Carol said, dropping her voice despite the fact that the twins couldn't possibly hear her over the commotion they were making, "maybe you could see if there's anything online about the body found at the school."

"I could," Harvey said, drawing out the words. "But do you want that to be a topic of discussion now? Jenny and Craig will be here shortly, and I thought you hoped Jenny wouldn't find out about your night sleuthing."

Carol sighed deeply. Her natural curiosity and her desire to avoid a lecture from Jenny were at war. Plus, she felt responsible somehow. It wasn't that she'd contributed to the poor woman's death, of course, but she'd been there. Surely that meant she should *do* something, even if the something was only keeping up with the news about it. On top of that, she still hadn't decided if the twins should avoid the school for a few days.

"Hush, Gavin," Maisie said to her brother with her hands on her hips. "You made Grandma sigh. Wait until Mom finds out."

"I did not make Grandma sigh," Gavin insisted. "You did that."

"Neither of you did it," Carol said as she reached over the twins to unlock the door. "Let's get inside before we freeze."

"I'm going to check on the girls," Harvey said, already on his way to the chicken coop.

"I'm going with Grandpa!" Gavin yelled.

Maisie rolled her eyes. "Boys. I'll help you get lunch ready, Grandma."

"I appreciate that." Carol also appreciated the warmth of the house after the bitter cold outside. January sometimes surprised them with the occasional temperate day, but for anyone born and bred in Michigan, warm in winter was anything above freezing.

She helped Maisie out of her coat and mittens, then they set to work getting the meal on the table. Not for the first time, Carol appreciated her slow cooker for the ease of having something hot ready on a cold day.

Maisie stood on her tiptoes to try to peer through the clear lid of the slow cooker. "What's cooking, Grandma? It smells yummy."

"Beef stew," Carol said. "And some yeast rolls from the bakehouse. I want to pop them in the oven so they'll be warm. That way, the butter will melt on them."

Maisie clutched her stomach. "Talking about it is making my tummy rumble. It wants to eat right now."

Carol reached into the refrigerator and fetched out a carrot stick. "Here. This will give your stomach something else to think about."

Maisie squinted doubtfully at the carrot. "I'll try, but it's going to know this isn't a buttered roll."

Carol chuckled, then started at the sound of the door opening and the clatter of feet. It sounded like more commotion than Harvey and Gavin could manage on their own, so Carol headed for the door, certain she'd find Jenny and Craig there. She did, but the moment Jenny spotted her mother, a disapproving scowl crossed her face.

Jenny pointed at Carol with the leather gloves in her hand. "We need to talk."

"Can you do it after lunch?" Craig asked. He held up a casserole dish wrapped in a towel. "I'm starving."

"Me too," Gavin said.

"And me!" Maisie announced from Carol's side. "Sorry, Grandma, but the carrot didn't give my tummy enough to think about."

"It can wait," Jenny said, but her frown only softened, not vanishing completely. Still, the process of getting the food out helped. With four adults in the kitchen, they bumped into one another quite a bit. Finally, the twins hauled their parents to the tall windows overlooking the loch to hunt for lake monsters.

"What's Jenny mad about?" Carol whispered to Harvey as she lined the bread basket with a cloth before dumping in the warm rolls.

Harvey shrugged. "At a guess, news of last night's activity has reached her."

Carol winced. *Hopefully not.* By the time they settled down to eat, Jenny was smiling again, so Carol had high hopes that everything was going to be okay. The beef stew she'd put together with Harvey before church was perfect for the cold day, tasty and filling. As usual, Laura's rolls were light as a dream. They barely had room afterward for the deep-dish fruit cobbler Jenny had made, but somehow they all managed to have a helping.

Harvey pushed away from the table and groaned. "I volunteer for dishes. I need to stand up so my food can fall down into my legs."

Maisie giggled. "It doesn't work that way, Grandpa."

"Right," Gavin chimed in. "We learned all about it in school."

"You two can educate me while we clear the table," Harvey said.

Craig hopped up and began piling dishes. "I'll help so the twins don't talk you to death."

"Good," Jenny said, her face now serious. "That way Mom and I can talk."

"Uh-oh," Maisie said.

Carol suspected Maisie had summed it up perfectly. As she suspected from Jenny's attitude, her daughter had gotten a text from a fellow teacher about the night before. Carol wondered aloud if the informant could be Byron Quayle, but Jenny refused to be drawn off topic by revealing her source.

"Mom," she said, "as you're well aware, it worries me to death when you get involved in dangerous escapades."

"Your father was with me," Carol said. "Why aren't you yelling at him?"

"Because I know who the ringleader is when it comes to these things. I know you informed him you were going to do it no matter how he felt about it, and he decided he'd better come along to watch your back." Jenny sighed deeply, reminding Carol of her own reaction earlier. "I don't expect you'll leave this matter alone now that you're in it, but please promise me you'll be careful—and that you won't rush off on your own."

Carol patted her daughter's arm. "I'm not rushing anywhere. I doubt I'll be involved at all now that the police are handling it. They do a fine job."

"That should be reassuring," Jenny said. "But somehow it isn't. Maybe because, as fine a job as you say they do, that's never stopped you from staying involved before."

Carol laughed. "Well, be reassured. I'm going to be fine. I'm more concerned about the twins at the school. Do you think they should take a few days off?"

"I'll consider it." Jenny leaned back. "You want to know what I think?"

"I have a feeling you're going to tell me regardless."

Jenny ignored her comment. "I think you should go on the fishing trip with Dad. It'll keep you out of trouble. By the time you get home, this will probably be all settled."

"How did you know about your father's fishing trip?" Carol asked suspiciously.

"I should go check on the twins." Jenny hopped up and rushed to the kitchen. Carol followed, but her thoughts were on Harvey, who was going to get a talk of his own.

Monday morning, Carol headed into work earlier than usual, fuming a bit. She'd tried to discuss Harvey's enlisting Jenny to convince Carol that the fishing trip was a good idea, but Harvey had turned it around to pressure her to talk to Molly and Laura about it. They hadn't ended up fighting, exactly, but the matter wasn't settled either.

"The problem," Carol said aloud as she drove, "is that Harvey and I are both stubborn." And to that problem, she had no solution at all.

With her early start, Carol expected to beat Laura and Molly to work. Instead, Carol found both of her friends already busy in the Bread on Arrival kitchen.

"Aren't you both early birds today?" Carol asked.

"We're both eager to talk about Saturday," Molly said. "And since you're early too, I assume you feel the same way."

Carol didn't tell them that her earliness was mostly fueled by mild marital discord. Her friends would fret and ask her dozens of questions. Instead, she said, "The discovery of a body was mentioned on the Sunday evening news. They were very vague, barely admitting someone in Loch Mallaig had died under potentially mysterious circumstances."

"The only surprising part of that is that Loch Mallaig was mentioned at all," Molly grumbled. "Why does a dead body have to appear before the news pays any attention to us? There's more to us than that."

"The coverage was disappointing," Laura said. "I hoped they'd identify the person. Not even the *Crown Press News* had the poor woman's name, and they aren't exactly known for their discretion."

Carol snorted. "Nor for their strict adherence to research and facts. I had thought you might know more, Molly."

"Me?" Molly squeaked. "Why?"

"Because you had a Piping Yoopers practice yesterday," Carol replied, referring to the local bagpipers group Molly was in along with many others, including Fergus, Mayor Tavish Calhoun, and Officer Greer Anderson. "And I know Greer rarely misses a rehearsal."

Molly gave a wounded sniff. "She missed yesterday's, and she hasn't responded to my calls. I bet she's avoiding me because she thinks I'll pump her for information."

"Not a totally unfair assumption," Laura said.

"No, not totally," Molly admitted.

Laura paused in the middle of dumping flour into a large mixer and gave them a sly grin. "We might be able to learn something when we go in to give our formal statements. The sooner the better."

"Officer Drummond said he'd call us in when he's ready," Carol said.

"But should we make him wait?" Laura asked. "Isn't it our civic duty to go over there? We could even go together. Hamish is coming in this morning, so if we get all the bread baked, we could leave the shop in his crabby, capable hands."

"Fergus and I made plans to go together," Molly said. "I figured the shop could spare me since January is always so slow."

"Slow is relative," Carol said. "We have lines at the counter most mornings. They may not be long lines, but think of all the businesses around here that close all winter long. We don't need to do that, and it's all due to our baking and Molly's great promotions."

That settled the conversation for a while, and they focused as much as possible on the morning prep. When the time came to open, Carol volunteered to wait on customers until Hamish arrived to start his shift. They found a few people already waiting, and though they never exactly had a crowd, they did have a steady stream of patrons.

Carol heard a little speculative chatter about the mysterious death, but no one peppered her with questions. It was clear that, so far, the presence of the three bakers was not part of the gossip surrounding the woman's death.

Thank goodness for that at least, she thought.

"I bet someone went out without enough clothes," one older man announced. "Probably some teenager. They worry more about being 'cool' than staying warm. Likely froze herself to death."

"It's still awful," the man's wife chided. "Poor thing."

Carol filled mugs with coffee and plated scones for the two of them, choosing not to comment on their supposition. She knew there was no way the information wouldn't leak eventually, and then she'd be busy enough responding to impertinent questions. She didn't need to borrow trouble.

She handed over the older couple's breakfast, and they carried it to one of the rustic tables near the fireplace. It was the warmest spot, considering how often the door opened and let in the cold.

The bell over the door jingled, and Raimie and Kendra entered. A glance at the clock told Carol it was getting close to the start of classes at the elementary school. The two young women were cutting it close. They hurried to the counter.

"What can I get you?" Carol asked.

"Two coffees to go, please," Kendra said. Then she dropped her voice to a bare whisper and added, "Have you heard who the dead woman was?"

"No, and neither has Laura or Molly." Carol began dispensing coffee into two cups.

Raimie leaned over the counter to whisper, "Kendra said you saw someone inside the school? Is that who died?"

"I can't say for sure, but probably not," Carol answered as she finished filling the first cup. "It was forty-five minutes at most between when Fergus saw the person in the hallway and when we discovered the poor woman outside. I don't think that's nearly enough time, not from what the emergency worker said. Besides, Fergus said her skin was already cold."

Raimie was visibly relieved, and Kendra gave her assistant a knowing smile. "I told you."

"I know," Raimie said. "But all day yesterday, I was so worried that somehow I'd gotten you there, and you'd accidentally chased someone outside to freeze."

"I don't believe you have any reason to feel guilty," Carol said, snapping plastic lids on the two coffees before sliding them across the counter to the women.

Raimie gave her a weak smile and picked up her coffee. Kendra grabbed hers and handed over some folded bills. "We have to run. I don't want to be late, especially with the principal so unhappy with us."

Raimie bobbed her head. "She called every teacher at the school yesterday and said she expects zero talk about the body from anyone."

"That sounds like a bit of an overreaction," Carol said. "We're not talking about a pricey private school that depends on tuition money from students to survive. But I understand not wanting something so unpleasant hashed out in front of the children, of course."

Kendra rolled her eyes. "Some bosses love being controlling." She sipped her coffee, then saluted Carol with the cup. "This is delicious. Gotta run."

Carol watched the teachers leave and wondered about the principal's concerns. Was Mrs. Dour controlling? Perhaps that was it, but maybe her reasons were exactly what she said, and she was trying to do her best for the school and the community. With a mental shrug, Carol began straightening up the displays until the next customers came in. She knew it wouldn't be long.

Carol had just finished tidying the bagels when Molly burst wide-eyed from the hallway that led to the kitchen and rushed to Carol's side.

"Greer finally called me," Molly murmured urgently. "We have to give statements as soon as possible." She dropped her voice still further, though her eyes grew even wider. "That woman's death wasn't an accident. She was murdered!"

7

Carol shivered and pulled her wool scarf up to cover more of her face as she strode along the sidewalk. The walk had seemed like a good idea in the warm kitchen of Bread on Arrival, when she'd thought the journey would give her a chance to order her thoughts and prepare for her statement. She wasn't nervous, but she didn't want to forget anything either.

Once Hamish had arrived for work, Carol and her friends decided on the best order for heading to town hall, which housed the police department. Even if Molly hadn't been committed to waiting for Fergus, the Bakehouse Three couldn't have gone together, especially after a rush order had come in that Laura needed to work on. Ultimately, Laura elected to go last, and Carol headed out into the cold.

Smart thinking, she chided herself as she hunched inside her coat and tried to pick up her pace. She didn't dare move too fast. The town was good about keeping sidewalks free of snow, but it was still tricky. Patches of nearly invisible ice could be anywhere.

Blinking her stinging eyes, Carol tried to distract herself by appreciating that it truly was a beautiful day. The sun was shining, and when she stood still for a moment and tilted her face toward it with eyes closed, she could feel faint warmth on her skin, reminding her that spring would begin eventually. Around her, the sidewalks were mostly quiet, with the majority of people choosing to run their errands from the comfort of their warm cars.

She crossed onto Highland Street, where the chilly breeze off the lake no longer pushed her from behind and instead added to the sting in her eyes as it chilled one side of her face more than the other. She hadn't thought it possible for her skin to feel colder. At least the Loch Mallaig town hall was barely a block away.

She finally reached town hall and stepped inside. The warmth that enveloped her like a hug made her chuckle to herself. *You'd think I'd crossed the country in a covered wagon instead of walking a few blocks.*

The police receptionist, Wilma Guthrie, sat behind the counter, her cell phone pressed to her ear. Carol suppressed an eye roll at the sight of the woman, knowing Wilma spent much of her work time collecting and passing on gossip. Still, there was no other way to get to give her statement, so Carol marched up to the desk.

Wilma fixed her sharp, blue eyes on Carol and quickly ended her call. "Carol," Wilma said brightly, fluffing her teased red hair as she spoke. "It's always good to see you."

"Thanks, Wilma. I'm here to speak to Officer Drummond. Is he around?" Carol knew she should simply say she was there to make a statement, since she wasn't sure Officer Drummond was the one she needed to see, but she preferred not to give Wilma even that much information.

"I'll check," Wilma said. "Business or personal?"

"He'll know what it's about," Carol said, hoping her tight expression appeared enigmatic instead of annoyed.

Visibly disappointed that Carol hadn't been more forthcoming, Wilma picked up the phone on her desk and made a quick call. She dropped the receiver into the cradle with slightly more vigor than absolutely necessary. "Officer Drummond is on his way."

Moments later, a door near the reception desk opened, and Officer Drummond gestured to Carol. She followed him on a weaving path through desks to the interview rooms beyond.

"I wasn't certain who would be taking my statement," she said, "but I felt sure that you'd know."

"It won't be me," the officer said. "The deputy chief is running this investigation, and he wants to take the statements since he wasn't there for our initial conversation at the scene."

"It's always nice to see Deputy Chief Gillespie," Carol said.

Officer Drummond chuckled. "And I'm sure he feels the same way about you."

Carol realized he thought she was kidding. In truth, Carol admired the deputy chief. He was smart and fair and had always treated her respectfully. "Have things been stressful around here?" she asked.

"Isn't it always?" he replied wryly. "But yeah, it's been a bit above average. The department is getting a ton of pressure to solve the crime quickly and quietly."

"Where does the pressure come from?"

"The mayor mostly, but it didn't start there. He's getting hammered himself."

"By whom?"

The officer shook his head. "I can't say, and you're entirely too easy to talk to, Mrs. MacCallan."

"Thank you, I think," Carol said, and quickly added, "I imagine the pressure is coming from the elementary school principal."

"I can't say." But the officer's eyes told Carol plenty. She had hit the nail on the head.

When she came through the door of the interview room, the deputy chief was already seated, but he rose immediately to greet her. He was tall, almost looming compared to Carol, and had straight, black hair and light brown skin. His coloring and impressive cheekbones were a gift from his Chippewa mother and his striking hazel eyes were the only visible genetic contribution from his Scottish father. "Thank you for coming in so quickly," he said in greeting. "I appreciate not having to track you down."

"I want to do anything I can to help the investigation," Carol said after she'd shaken his hand.

He waved her to a chair on the other side of the table. "Please sit, and tell me about the events of Saturday night. I don't think you need any prompting, so tell me in your own way, whatever you remember. Don't hold anything back. You never know what could be important."

Carol ran through the night as analytically as she could. It was easy enough until she came to the moment they'd found the woman. Her voice hitched, and she couldn't go on.

"Take your time," the deputy chief said, his eyes gentle. "It must have been shocking."

Carol blinked away the tears. "It broke my heart," she admitted, her voice still uneven. "No one should end up on the cold pavement behind a dumpster like garbage."

"I agree with that," the deputy chief said. "I'm interested in the encounter with the disappearing intruder. Do you have any theories about how the person got away?"

"Some. The tracks in the snow I mentioned suggest to me that the person left through the basement."

"And entered the same way?"

"Maybe, though the custodian says that's not possible, and we couldn't gain entry through that door when we tried," she explained. "But I don't know how else it could have happened, unless the person was already in there somehow. That was Molly's theory. I assume you have examined the school yourself, with the body found so close by. Did you uncover anything?"

Gillespie's expression gave nothing away. "Let's stick to what *you* know."

"You'll hear more about the intruder when Molly and Fergus come in for their statements," Carol said. "They're the ones who actually saw the intruder, unless the intruder really was the poor woman we found in the parking lot. In that case, we all saw her. Is it true that she was killed on purpose? Did someone hit her with the dumpster lid?"

"We aren't here for me to answer questions," he reminded her again. "But I do admire your persistence. I always have."

She grinned at him. "Admire and enjoy aren't the same thing, are they?"

"Not quite." Deputy Chief Gillespie leaned forward and rested his elbows on the table between them. "Mrs. MacCallan, I am interested in your thoughts, as I've found them helpful in the past."

"Oh?" she said lightly. "You haven't always acted like it."

"If you can't beat 'em, join 'em, as they say," the deputy chief replied. "But seriously, what do you think?"

"The intruder and the dead woman must be linked, even if they aren't the same person," Carol said. "It feels too coincidental otherwise. But I don't see how the break-ins could prompt a murder. They've mainly been frightening for the teachers, not lucrative for the intruder, unless there's something I don't know. The person mostly stole old clothes, snacks, and some old mats."

"Yes, I have a list." Gillespie flattened his hands against the table with a growl of frustration. "There are a lot of odd pieces here, and I don't know what to make of them."

"Maybe it would help if we knew who the victim was," Carol suggested. "Do you know?"

"Yes, but that isn't information we're sharing with the public," he said. "We never do until the victim's next of kin are notified, and that's proving a bit difficult."

"That was a quick identification," Carol said. "I assume the woman was local?"

He shook his head. "No comment."

Carol gave up, realizing she'd get nothing on the victim's identity from the deputy chief. That didn't mean she couldn't get it another way, but she'd have to give some thought as to how.

The deputy chief wrapped up the interview and switched off the recorder that had been running. "I'll have someone type this up and run it by the bakehouse for you to sign, along with the other statements we'll collect from the rest of you today."

"I hope I helped," Carol said, rising from her chair.

He stood as well. "Adding pieces to the puzzle always helps. Now we have to figure out where they fit."

He thanked her warmly and walked her to the door to the reception area. He left Carol to open it and head through. She suspected the deputy chief's manners would normally have prompted him to open it for her, but he probably didn't want to be caught by any lurking reporters. Despite her penchant for gossip, Wilma normally kept the reception area clear of the media, but better safe than sorry.

Instead of reporters on the prowl, Carol found Molly and Fergus, who stood when they saw her. "Was it terrible?" Molly asked.

Carol stepped close and dropped her voice, not wanting to add to Wilma's gossip reservoir. "No, but it'll be Deputy Chief Gillespie asking questions. He was particularly interested in what you may have seen of the intruder."

"We won't be able to tell much," Fergus said. "The person appeared to be wearing a lot of layers. Of course, the poor woman by the dumpster was too."

"Do you think it could have been the same person?" Carol asked, hoping Fergus had a more definitive answer than Molly had.

"I've asked myself that question a lot, and I know Molly has too," he said. "Honestly, Carol, I don't know. Maybe? The person inside moved so fast. We didn't get much more than an impression. And no guess as to the gender, though I had the same problem with the woman outside. Even with having to loosen some clothing to do CPR, I didn't have a good guess as to whether it was a man or a woman. All I saw were layers and layers of worn clothing."

"So we saw two thickly bundled figures, suggesting both people—if there were two—planned to be out in the cold for a long time," Carol said. "You'd swelter indoors wearing that many clothes. I've already gotten hot with my coat on, and I put it on maybe a minute ago, when he said I could go."

"Maybe the poor woman didn't have a warm place to be," Molly said softly, and it was plain that she was feeling the same pain they had talked about earlier, of thinking that Loch Mallaig had failed the woman somehow, that *they* had failed her.

"We didn't know her," Fergus said gently. "Sometimes people don't ask for help."

Molly took a shuddering breath. "You're right."

The door to the reception area opened again, and Greer Anderson poked her head out and called for Molly and Fergus. She also waved at Carol. Carol waved back, then hustled out of the police headquarters before Wilma could try pumping her for gossip.

The bitter cold outside made Carol gasp. How did it always manage to be such a shock to her system? As she headed to the bakery, she reminded herself that it was good that she had walked. She needed to be aware of how bitter the winter could get. Who else would be out in this with no warm bakehouse waiting at the end? The thought made her shudder.

As she thought about the cozy bakery, she wondered if there was somewhere else where cold people could take refuge. The church, of course. St. Andrew's Church even had The Closet, which offered clothes and household items to anyone in need. Laura volunteered there when her schedule allowed. This time of year, The Closet supplied a lot of winter clothes. But Carol also knew that not everyone saw the church as a refuge of comfort and acceptance. Some had had bad experiences with other churches that kept them away from all of them now.

In that case, where would someone go? Then she thought of something she'd read in the paper in Pittsburgh years before about homeless people congregating in the public libraries in the winter because they were free and warm. The piece she'd read had been a letter to the editor complaining about how the homeless took up all the comfortable chairs. Carol had been disgusted by the attitude. Still, it did leave her to wonder: Could the victim have spent time in the Loch Mallaig Public Library for the same reason? She should ask Grizela Duff, the head librarian.

The thought brought a fresh shiver. Grizela was difficult at the best of times. However, once the bakehouse closed for the day, she would consider it.

She realized that she was walking past St. Andrew's, and she stopped to wonder if it would be worthwhile to stop in. She could ask Laura, of course, but here she was, right outside and brimming with questions. Did they keep any records of people who'd gotten clothes? That sounded unlikely. It would be intrusive. Still, someone may have noticed the woman.

Carol was still mulling it over when a car roared up beside her, nearly climbing the curb as it approached. She barely had time to shriek when its horn blared.

8

Even as she jumped from the sound, Carol recognized Harvey's Jeep Cherokee. She put her hands on her hips and scowled at it. The driver's side door swung open and Harvey climbed out and hurried toward her, his expression sheepish.

"I'm sorry, honey," he said. "I didn't mean to scare you. I saw you and thought I'd ask you to come with me to the town hall while I gave my statement. Then I can drive you to the bakehouse in a nice, warm vehicle."

"I'm fine," she replied firmly. "I was thinking that I ought to go ask Grizela about the woman who'd died. I remembered reading that homeless people sometimes go to public libraries to warm up."

"That's true. There was a bit of a brouhaha about it some years ago in Pittsburgh." He gestured toward the church. "So, if you were heading to the library, why were you standing at the church?"

"I also thought about The Closet and wondered if the woman had come here."

"So you're going to make two stops?" he asked. "Want me to come along?"

Carol cast a glance toward the church. "You can come with me to St. Andrew's. With Molly and Fergus ahead of you, you'll have to wait to give your statement anyway."

"Then I am at your disposal." Harvey crooked an elbow, and she smiled as she accepted it.

St. Andrew's was a classic village church with a small but meticulously maintained cemetery behind it. Carol and Harvey headed into the building through a side entrance that led directly to the public area of The Closet. Clothing was sorted, cleaned, and mended in a private room, and Carol suspected that was where long-term records might be kept. Carol waved at the volunteer on duty and breezed past her. She'd learned long ago that if you acted as if you were on a mission, people would often let you pass without a question.

Carol was startled to find that the processing area wasn't empty. Reverend Stuart Findlay, a tall, sturdy man of about sixty, stood next to a long table, carefully folding sweaters. The sleeves on his shirt were rolled up, and the humidity in the air from the washer and dryer had given his dark hair a slight curl. Nearby, his wife, Bonnie, perched on a stool with a sweater in her lap. She wore her strawberry-blonde hair in a bob, which was held away from her face by a headband.

They both beamed a welcome at Carol and Harvey. "How nice to see you," Reverend Findlay said. "Please don't tell me I've forgotten a meeting."

"No," Carol assured him. "This is an impromptu visit. I had some questions about the clothing—or rather, about those the clothing helps."

"I mostly handle that side and work with our volunteers, including Laura," Bonnie said. "Stuart specializes in spiritual needs."

The reverend chuckled. "And yet here I am on a Monday morning, folding clothes."

"Only because you hate to see anyone working without chipping in," his wife said with a smile. "What did you want to know, Carol?"

Carol explained about how they'd found the woman behind the dumpster and her layers of worn clothing. The Findlays' faces grew grave.

"How horrible." Bonnie's blue eyes swam with tears. "No one should end up like that."

"My thoughts exactly," Carol said solemnly, and Harvey put a comforting arm around her shoulders. "Do you think she may have come here to get warm clothes? Maybe with someone else?"

The reverend furrowed his brow. "We couldn't tell you about specific people who use our services. If anyone thought we'd gossip about them, they wouldn't come here anymore, and we couldn't minister to their needs."

"I'm hoping to learn what happened to the woman," Carol said.

"And I know that comes from your kind heart, but we cannot bend on this." The reverend exchanged a look with his wife, and she nodded her agreement.

"We can't do anything that might deter people from coming," Bonnie said. "There is more need than people realize. We get so many donations, but we still give away nearly every coat and sweater each year, and so often the people in need cannot always find their size among our donations."

"What sizes are you usually short on?" Harvey asked.

"Larger ones, mainly," Bonnie said. "We get a great many donations of children's clothes, since kids often outgrow a coat before they wear it out. It's not the same for adult clothes, though. Loch Mallaig's own Fair Knitting Ladies donate mittens and hats and scarves every year, as you well know, Carol, and they are much appreciated. However, sweaters and coats for adults are harder to come by. Especially the larger sizes, since they can layer over other clothes."

Carol thought of how proud she was to contribute to the local knitting group's charity offerings, but they'd never thought about doing sweaters, which took longer, used more complicated patterns, and consumed more yarn. Perhaps the club should rethink their approach.

Bonnie pressed her hands down on the sweater in her lap, her eyes full of curiosity. "You know, Laura could have told you most of this."

"I'm sure," Carol said. "But the questions came to me when I was outside."

Reverend Findlay laughed. "You sound like Bonnie. The second she thinks of something, she wants to act on it."

"And you love it," his wife said, her expression mischievous.

"I do," he agreed.

Carol gently pulled the conversation back on course. "The woman at the school wore many layers, and it made me wonder if she was homeless."

"Many of our poorer residents wear a lot of layers," Bonnie said. "They can't afford proper heat, and some of the older homes aren't insulated well, either."

Carol felt Harvey's arm tighten around her. He always knew when she was distressed. "If the police showed you a photo of the woman," he said, "would you be able to say if she'd come here? After all, she's not going to mind about her privacy so much anymore."

The reverend didn't act any happier, but he didn't resist. "I would help the police however I can. But even so, I won't reveal any confidences of the living, not even to help the dead."

Carol studied the sweater Bonnie was mending, which had a long tear down the center. The sweaters the reverend was folding were also quite worn. At that moment, Carol decided to do a thorough search through the house for any warm clothes they didn't wear often. She knew she tended to hold on to clothes, especially those she thought she might wear eventually. *No more waiting for eventually when there are people in need right now.*

Bonnie must have misinterpreted Carol's musing because she laid a hand on her arm. "You do a lot for this community," she said. "Don't think it goes unnoticed. We all serve the Lord in our own way and our own calling. Don't ever beat yourself up because you don't do it all yourself. You have to make room for others to answer the call too."

"Thank you," Carol said. "But there's something my grandmother told me years ago too. Once you are aware of a problem, you must do what you can about it."

"As long as you make your choices wisely," Reverend Findlay put in. "Even good intentions can take a person on an impetuous and unwise journey."

"Wise words," Harvey said. "I should have them stitched on a pillow for Carol's side of the bed."

Carol thumped her husband lightly on the arm. "In which case I'll just put it on your side of the bed, and you can sleep in the guest room."

The Findlays laughed, and the reverend said, "Don't let my ramblings cause marital discord. It could affect people's trust in my marriage counseling."

"Not to worry," Harvey said. "I cause plenty of discord on my own."

"That you do," Carol agreed. She smiled at the other couple. "Thank you for your time and for giving me much to think about. I appreciate it."

She tugged Harvey through The Closet and into the cold again. She was almost inclined to think that the temperature dropped a bit each time she stepped outside, but she was fairly sure that was her imagination. "I'm going to the library now," she said. "You can head on to the police station."

"In for a penny, in for a pound," Harvey said. "As much as Grizela terrifies me, I'll give you a lift over."

"It's a few blocks," Carol said, though she was dreading all of them.

"More than enough in this weather." They'd reached the SUV, so Harvey opened her door with a flourish, making her chuckle. He really was a ham sometimes.

Once she was settled and Harvey was steering the Cherokee toward the library, Carol returned to her thoughts about warm clothes. "I have a sweater at home that I knit a while ago," she said. "It's plenty soft and warm, but it's too bulky for my style. When I tried it on, it made me look plump as a partridge."

"Certainly the fault of the sweater," he said seriously.

"Flatterer," she said. She appreciated that he acted as though she were still the college girl he'd fallen in love with, even if she saw a bit more padding and wrinkles in the mirror. "Anyway, I'd like to donate it to someone who needs the warmth. And I know I have some coats that I could give to the clothing program."

"As long as you don't give away my barn coat, I'm fine."

"You do know that we don't have a barn."

"Yes, but coop coat sounds silly. And I am not a silly man."

Carol swallowed a guffaw. "Oh, my mistake. Forgive me for implying such a thing."

The two-story brick building that housed the library came into view when they reached Balmoral Lane. Though one of the older buildings in Loch Mallaig, it had managed to stay solid and eternal instead of worn. Carol suspected the building wouldn't dare crumble or crack. The head librarian wouldn't approve. Carol would never speak such a fanciful theory aloud, but she felt it all the same.

They swung the SUV into the small parking lot, which was nearly full. Harvey managed to squeeze the SUV into a parking space about as far from the library's front door as possible.

"I'll be getting my walking in today," Carol said.

"Since I failed to save you from that, it's only fair that I suffer as well," Harvey said gravely.

Despite the number of patrons inside, it didn't take long to find Grizela Duff tutting over some worn books on a table. She peered up at Carol and Harvey as they approached her. "I imagine it's clear I'm busy."

"Fairly clear," Harvey acknowledged.

Grizela tapped a nearby book. "I have to decide which ones are worthy of repair and which need to be retired. Patrons should be more careful."

"Books are made to be loved," Carol said in a flash of bravery. She knew that disagreeing with Grizela meant she risked a thorough tongue lashing.

Instead, Grizela merely said, "Aye." She set down the book and waved at two chairs near the table. "Assuming the two of you won't go away until you say whatever's on your mind, you may as well sit."

Carol spoke even as she was slipping into the seat. "Do you get many patrons who come in to get out of the cold?"

The scowl Grizela gave her suggested the librarian seriously questioned Carol's intelligence. "As you may have noticed, it's January. Of course people come in to get out of the cold."

Carol chose not to react to Grizela's tone. She'd talked to the librarian enough to know that her constant grumpiness was nearly as much an act as Hamish's. Grizela was dedicated to the community, even though she sometimes thought they were all a bit dim. "Can you tell me if you've seen anyone unusually bundled? Dressed in many thick layers as if they expect to be out in the cold for long periods of time?"

"Tattered layers," Harvey added. "No real coat."

Grizela cut her eyes from Carol to Harvey and back again. Carol waited patiently under the other woman's shrewd gaze. She knew better than to show any sign of impatience. Finally, the librarian came to some kind of decision. "We get a few."

"Any women?" Carol asked. "I know at least one of the people we are searching for is a woman."

"Searching for?" Grizela crossed her arms. "Am I to assume you have good intentions for this woman? I will not send any of my patrons into the arms of trouble. And I don't indulge in gossip, as you are well aware."

"Which I appreciate and respect," Carol said. "We're trying to help."

"We do get two women in here," Grizela said finally. "Doris and Meg. They almost always come in together, usually as soon as the library opens." She harrumphed. "Doris always chooses romance novels. She parks in one of the chairs in the corner, away from everyone else, and reads half the day away."

Carol thought that sounded like a perfectly wonderful way to spend a winter day. "And Meg?"

"She goes straight to the periodicals," Grizela said. "She flips through the magazines. When they first started coming, some of the volunteers would linger around the magazines, thinking Meg might be inclined to tear them up. People do sometimes. But Meg is not stupid, and she got right snippy with the women for watching her. I don't blame her for disliking the spying, but Meg is a grouchy old thing, for sure."

Harvey barked a laugh, which he quickly smothered in a cough. Carol didn't blame him, but he earned a scowl from Grizela.

"Are they here now?" Carol asked.

The librarian shook her head, making her head of short gray curls bounce a bit. "Though that is strange for sure. They're generally here on Monday mornings."

"Do you know where they live?" Harvey asked. "Or their last names?"

"No clue," Grizela replied. "They've never signed up for a library card and do all their reading on the premises." Then she poked his arm with a bony finger. "Not that I'd tell you. That would be unprofessional, which you ought to know."

Harvey rubbed at his arm, though Carol doubted Grizela had done him much harm. "I know it now," he grumbled.

"If that's all, you two should be on your way." Grizela flapped a hand at them. "I need to get back to my work. Some of us can't lollygag the day away. I'm surprised to see a baker can."

Carol glanced at the large clock on the wall and yelped. "No," she said as she stood. "A baker can't. Thank you for your help."

Grizela harrumphed, already absorbed in the stack of books before her again.

Carol wove through the tables and shelves with Harvey, her mind racing. She had a strong hunch they'd just learned the names of both the intruder and the victim—Doris and Meg. But she had no idea which of the two had died on Saturday night. And how could she possibly find the survivor?

9

Back out in the cold, Carol noticed the weather had changed while they were inside. Clouds had rolled in and now tiny snowflakes fell lightly around them. She sometimes grumbled about the amount of snow they got each year, but the little girl inside her rejoiced at every swirling flake. She'd loved winter's magic as a child. She tightened the scarf around her neck and waved toward the street. "I can walk to the bakehouse from here," she told Harvey. "You should head on to police headquarters."

"I don't think so." Harvey guided her toward the Cherokee with a hand under her elbow. "You don't need to be out in the cold all day."

"I've hardly been in the cold all day," she said, "considering I keep ending up in warm buildings."

"Even worse," he said. "Jumping in and out so much is bad for you. Shocks your system and all."

"And for you?"

"I'm made of tough stuff. Now stop being contrary for the sake of it and let me drive you to work."

Carol was tempted to continue the protest purely out of stubbornness, but she was cold and getting to Bread on Arrival quicker would be fairer to Laura. Still, she made a point of giving a put-upon sigh as she let Harvey haul her along.

Harvey cranked up the heat as soon as he started the engine, though they'd been inside long enough that this merely meant they were blasted with more cold air. "When I talk to the police," he said,

"I'll throw out what we know about Doris and Meg and see if I can shock some more information out of them."

"Deputy Chief Gillespie took my statement, so I imagine he'll take yours. He's not easily rattled."

Harvey shrugged. "You never know."

They reached the bakehouse within a few minutes. Snow lay on the old Victorian's roof and clung to the black shutters, as well as the balcony railings on the wraparound porch. The flower beds near the front steps had vanished under mounds of white and probably wouldn't be seen again for months. Still, it was a lovely building in the falling snow, like an image from a vintage Christmas card. Every time she paused to take in the bakehouse, Carol got the same warm feeling of home that she experienced pulling up the drive to their beautiful log house.

She pulled herself from her reverie with some effort. "Somehow the distance to the bakery seemed much farther when I was walking." Carol leaned over and gave Harvey a peck on the cheek. "I'll see you at home this afternoon. Though you should feel free to call me if you learn anything."

"Sure thing." He squeezed her hand, then let go as she opened the door.

Carol hopped out and hurried in the front door. The gentle jingle of the bell over the door was nearly as welcoming as the warmth, which carried the scent of baked bread and treats. *No wonder we keep customers even in the winter. Coming through this door makes everything better.* The sensation was increased by the cozy charm of the customer area, from the well-kept wood floors to the rustic bistro tables, each with a Celtic knot carved into the top.

Carol headed for the counter, catching greetings from regular customers and replying with "*guid mornin*," as was her habit. The Scottish greeting was her way to remember her own Scottish grandparents on her father's side.

She greeted Hamish as well. He muttered something about how it must be nice to gad about on a busy day. She patted his arm. "Hello to you too," she said brightly before heading to the kitchen to find out what work awaited her.

Laura was bent over a row of cream puffs, carefully filling each one. Her face lit up when Carol walked in. "I'm so glad you're back. I was getting nervous about how long it was taking. I could almost picture the police grilling you with bright lights."

"No bright lights," Carol said as she tied on an apron. "Though they did bring out the big guns. Broderick Gillespie took my statement."

Laura whistled. "Wow, they are taking this poor woman's death very seriously."

"I'm glad," Carol said. "I don't want to live in a town where a death so horrible could be brushed aside simply because the victim was homeless." She checked the order list for what she needed to do next, then began gathering ingredients for a cake due for an afternoon pickup.

"He must have asked a lot of questions to keep you so long," Laura said.

"He was thorough, but I didn't come straight here. I thought I should see if I could learn the woman's identity. Assuming she was homeless or at least had fallen on hard times, I tried to imagine where she would go for help."

"Other than raiding the school for old clothes and treats?" Laura asked.

"I can't imagine the woman dressed herself with only elementary school lost-and-found items," Carol said, dumping flour into a bowl. "I thought of The Closet program at the church and the library."

"I can tell you about The Closet." Then Laura froze and gaped at Carol. "Wait a second. Did you question Grizela?"

"I had Harvey with me," Carol admitted. "Plus, Grizela's bark is worse than her bite."

"Doesn't mean I enjoy either one. So did you learn anything?"

Carol slumped a bit as she remembered. "I popped into the church since I was right there. I learned things you probably already know. Bonnie Findlay spends a lot of time mending the worn things donated. We ought to do better. Someone facing hard times shouldn't have to give up the right to decent clothes. In fact, it seems to me that the poor could use the morale boost more than anyone."

"I agree, which is why I volunteer there." Laura's tone was slightly strained by impatience, making Carol realize she'd wandered off topic.

"I also found out Grizela may have seen the woman, and possibly the person Fergus spotted inside too, assuming they're two different people. Apparently two women named Meg and Doris hang out at the library pretty regularly. What if one of them is the victim? Grizela said they are usually at the library as soon as it opens, but not today."

"That does sound overly coincidental, though you never know." Laura waved toward the kitchen doorway. "You should ask Hamish about the women. If they're local, he may know them. He certainly *thinks* he knows everyone in Loch Mallaig."

Carol considered that. It was a good idea, so as soon as her cake was in the oven, she washed her hands and went up front. No one stood in line at the counter, though several of the tables around the room were full. Hamish was cleaning the display glass.

"I have a question for you," she said.

He frowned at her. "I hope it's not, 'will you stay late,' because Joyce is expecting me to help watch the wee girls today."

Carol chuckled. "No. I wouldn't want to keep you from your

wife and granddaughters. I actually want to tap into your knowledge of Loch Mallaig residents."

The tall man brightened. "I do know most of the folk around here."

"I'm searching for more information about two women," Carol said. "Not young women, but I'm not sure of their ages. Could be close to fifty or as old as seventy, but I'm inclined to think younger."

Hamish cocked his head. "Nice job narrowing that down."

"I'm doing the best I can," Carol said. "They're both living hard, maybe even homeless. Their names are Meg and Doris. They've been spending a lot of their time at the library."

Hamish put away the cleaning cloth and scratched at his white beard as he thought. "You're not giving me a lot to go on." Then his eyes widened. "Those two names *do* stir a memory. You don't hear the name Doris much around here, so that's why I thought of these girls. I doubt it's them, though."

"What girls?" Carol asked.

"It was from a high school history class when I was a young teacher." He chuckled at the recollection. "I wasn't much older than the students, truth be told, but so full of my big ideas about teaching."

"I know what that's like," Carol said. She had her own memories of her first years teaching, and some of them made her cringe at how much she thought she knew.

"At any rate, I had three young hooligans in my class—Millie, Meg, and Doris. They were thick as thieves and twice as devilish."

That almost made Carol chuckle. She thought about herself, Molly, and Laura in college. They'd never gotten out of hand, but in the right light, the same could have been said of them a time or two.

Hamish shook his head. "Those girls were part of a particularly mischievous class. That's the year the football team put a cow in the principal's office as a joke. The poor cow apparently panicked at the sound of a floor polisher the school custodian was using right outside the office. When the custodian heard the mooing, he opened the principal's door and was trampled. The man was in the hospital for a long time, as I remember, and was never able to work at the school again."

"And you think the girls were involved somehow?" Carol asked.

"Nay, it was the football team. Everyone knew it, though no one could prove it. Still, there's nothing like a team of high school lads to encourage hijinks during the dull winter months here. And they couldn't have known the cow would hurt anyone. They were good kids, truly, only feeling their oats a bit."

"But the cow thing came up right after your mention of the girls," Carol said. "Is there a link?"

"A small one, yes. All three of the girls' families moved out of Loch Mallaig not long after. The football team's prank scared a lot of parents, making them worry about bad influences. And the girls did lead each other off on adventures of their own sometimes. The parents probably hoped separating them would help settle them down."

"So Meg and Doris didn't stay in Loch Mallaig," Carol said, disappointed.

"I'm afraid not." He offered an apologetic smile. "Sorry for the trip down memory lane. I didn't mean to get your hopes up."

"It's still not impossible," Carol insisted. "They could have come back. Do you know their last names?"

Hamish frowned for a moment, but shook his head. "I don't remember. A great many teenagers passed through my history classes. I imagine you could find out from old school yearbooks. Doesn't the library carry those? Though since they'd be more than fifty now, they're probably all married with new last names."

"Still worth checking into," Carol mused. She thanked him

warmly and headed for the kitchen. She was sure there was plenty to be done while her cake continued baking, and she should see if they had any online orders as well. The orders were down in the lull between holidays, but they still received a handful every week.

Carol found Molly and Fergus in the kitchen talking to Laura. "Have I missed the recounting of your experience at police headquarters?" Carol asked.

"I imagine it was a lot like yours," Molly said. "Harvey came in as we were leaving. He told us about your visit with Grizela and what you learned."

"I learned a little more from Hamish, actually," Carol said. She recounted Hamish's remarks about the three high school girls, Doris, Meg, and Millie. "I'll have to put Harvey on the scent to see if he can dig up what happened to the three of them."

"I remember those girls," Fergus said. "Everyone called them the Wild'uns. They weren't in any of my classes, but everyone knew about them. They were a morality tale for my mother. Actually, Mom had a lot of morality tales from those high school years."

"Hamish told me about the cow in the principal's office too," Carol said.

Fergus winced. "I had nothing to do with that, though I knew guys on the football team, of course. I was more of a runner. No one hit you while you did that." His face brightened. "Actually, you all met one of the guys from the football team."

"We did?" Carol said.

"The emergency tech from Saturday night, Ballard Maddox. He was huge then, a real star. He was even being scouted by a couple colleges. He didn't end up going though."

"I noticed you chatting with him," Carol said. "Do you know him well?"

"Not really," Fergus admitted. "We haven't kept up, though I recognized him when I saw him. Saturday night wasn't a time for us to play catch-up, of course."

"Do you think he would have known Doris, Meg, or Millie?" Carol asked.

"Probably, but he wouldn't have recognized the person on the ground as one of those girls. I didn't. I do know that the woman we found wasn't Doris."

"Why?" Laura asked, pausing in the middle of rolling out pie dough.

"Doris was African-American," Fergus said. "And the woman we found was pale as a ghost. Actually, Doris was the only one of the Wild'uns that I knew at all. She was a little shy, which the other two were very much not. Her dad worked at Castleglen."

"He did?" Molly gaped at him, and Carol didn't blame her. Fergus was proving to be an unexpected fount of information. "What did he do?"

"This and that," Fergus said. "My dad always said Daniel Layville was the best handyman he'd ever had. He was upset when the family moved away."

Carol gasped. "Layville? Like Kendra Layville, the teacher from the elementary school?"

"Oh," Fergus said. "I didn't make the connection, but yes, the same name."

"It could be a coincidence," Laura suggested.

"Anything's possible," Carol agreed, "but the coincidences are beginning to lay thick on the ground here. I know one thing for certain. I need to make a school visit."

10

After Fergus left to resume his own work at Castleglen, Carol made sure they didn't have any orders she needed to bake for. Then she began gathering ingredients for sugar cookies.

"What are those for?" Molly asked.

"I don't want to go to the school empty-handed," Carol explained. "I thought frosted sugar cookies might sweeten my way."

"I would certainly spill all my secrets for a good cookie," Molly said.

"Not me," Laura mused as she wiped down the table where she'd been working. "I don't spill secrets for anything less than a torte."

Carol unwrapped a stick of softened butter and dropped it into the bowl. She poured the sugar on top of that and started the mixer to cream them. "What do you guys think?" she asked, raising her voice to be heard over the whir. "Could the Doris that has been hanging out at the library be a relative of Kendra's?"

"I doubt it," Molly said. "I mean, would you let a relative live rough when you had the power to help them?"

"Sometimes people won't let you help them. One thing I've learned from volunteering at The Closet is that people can be proud," Laura said. "And what if the woman is dangerous? What if whatever happened to Meg was because of a falling-out with Doris? Assuming, of course, that the woman we found *was* Meg. We are making a lot of leaps here."

Carol stopped the mixer to scrape down the sides of the bowl. "You're right. I shouldn't jump to conclusions. Let's talk about something cheerier—or at least something we can act on. I was really sad to see the state of some of the donations at The Closet this morning, and Bonnie Findlay said they have trouble getting clothes in larger sizes. I want to do something for The Closet here at the bakehouse. Laura volunteers, but surely there's something we could do as a business. Maybe we could inspire people to give sweaters and coats they don't wear that aren't quite so tattered."

Molly tilted her head thoughtfully to one side for a few moments, then she perked up. "What if we gave them something in exchange if they bring in a nice coat or sweater? We could give them something warm when they give something warm to the church."

"A cup of coffee or cocoa?" Laura asked.

"Perfect," Molly said. "We can call it Sweet Gifting. We give them something nice and warm when they give us something nice and warm."

"I like it," Laura agreed. "We could put out a nice big box for the donations."

Carol wrinkled her nose. "Dumping them in a box reminds me too much of the idea of clothes being thrown away. We really want to push the giving of nice things."

Molly's eyes lit up. "We can borrow a rolling clothes rack from the community center coat check. That way, people can hang up their donations instead of tossing them in a box. This is going to be so fun."

"We'll have to move some of the tables a little closer together to make room for a clothing rack, but it could work," Laura said. "I vote in favor. I would anyway since it'll help The Closet, but this is really a great idea."

"I also vote in favor," Carol agreed.

As if demanding that he be given a vote as well, Angus gave a sharp bark from upstairs in Molly's apartment. "Someone must be feeling neglected. The barking lot is a little cold this time of year and not many pups visit him there," Molly said, referring to the outdoor area Angus could access from her apartment, where patrons could leave well-behaved dogs to play while they enjoyed the bakehouse. "I'd better go up and remind him that he's my favorite dog in the world. While I'm there, I can work on this promotion idea." She grinned. "I can't wait."

As Carol watched her go, she realized she was happy about it as well. *At least we're moving forward on one front.* She continued work on her cookies and hoped they'd soon be moving forward on both.

Because she didn't want to miss Kendra at the school, Carol left the bakehouse before closing with the box of cookies in hand. Laura and Molly assured her they didn't mind tidying up for the day without her.

Carol took her car to keep the cookies safe, though she also had to admit that she'd had enough walking in the cold for one day. The drive took a little longer than usual since she was driving into school pickup traffic and buses. Still, she managed to find Kendra alone in her classroom, getting ready to leave for the day.

"How nice to see you," Kendra said with a wide smile.

Carol held out the cookies. "I made these to restock your snack supply. They aren't gluten- or dairy-free, but they *are* nut-free. I can make another batch without gluten or dairy, if you'd want. They require more careful prep and these were a sudden idea."

"These are wonderful," Kendra assured her. "I would be so grateful if you'd do the gluten-free and dairy-free as well. I can share them with the other teachers. None of us have restocked our treat supplies, and I know yours will be better than anything we can get at the store."

"I'll be glad to make some." Carol paused a moment before continuing. "Do you mind if I ask you a question? Were you born in Loch Mallaig?"

Kendra blinked in confusion at the apparent topic change. "No, I was born in Marquette. But my mom and my grandparents were from Loch Mallaig. In fact, that's why I'm here. My grandfather spoke of this town often. He loved it and made it sound like paradise. When a teaching job opened up here, I jumped at it. And after hearing Grandpa's stories, I do almost feel as if it's my hometown too."

Carol felt a flutter of excitement. So far this fit well. "Is your mother's name Doris, by any chance?"

Kendra's expression radiated curiosity. "Yes, her name was Doris. How did you know?"

"Was?"

A flicker of sadness passed over the young teacher's face. "My mom and dad died in a car accident when I was only a toddler. I don't remember them at all, though my grandparents had photos, of course, and stories."

"Oh, I'm so sorry," Carol said.

"It was a long time ago," Kendra said, her tone still sad. "I wish I remembered them more, but Grandma said it might be for the best. She said you can't grieve for what you don't know, but I'm not sure."

"I disagree with that idea," Carol said. "You can grieve for what could have been."

"I try not to dwell on it, honestly. Grandpa said sometimes grief can take up so much of your heart, there's no room for anything else. Anyway, I didn't suffer much. My grandparents are the best people in the world, and they spoiled me rotten."

"They sound lovely," Carol agreed.

"They are. They even officially adopted me. That's why I'm a Layville instead of a Barnside, which was my father's last name."

Carol hoped her disappointment didn't show. Clearly the Meg and Doris from the library weren't the ones from Hamish and Fergus's memories since Doris Layville had died. Still, the coincidence was hard to dismiss. "Your grandparents did a fine job raising you," Carol said finally. "I know the twins both think the world of you."

"They're great kids." Kendra smiled. "My classroom would be so dull without them."

Carol laughed, not doubting the truth of that statement. The twins livened up every place they went.

"Why did you want to know about my background?" Kendra asked.

"Someone mentioned your mother's name to me today," Carol said. "And it left me wondering if you were related." She chuckled. "I'm afraid I suffer from insatiable curiosity worse than the elephant's child in the Kipling story."

Kendra grinned at the reference. "Be careful. I hear that can lead to a long nose."

Carol excused herself so Kendra could finish her preparations to leave. She knew how tired she used to be at the end of a day of teaching and didn't want to keep the young woman. In all honesty, Carol longed to be home herself. She felt a deep weariness pass over her as she climbed into her car.

"Maybe I did walk too much in the cold today," she said aloud, but she suspected the sadness of Meg's death—if it had been Meg—still weighed on her too. As she drove, she revisited the odd coincidence of hearing of two possibly homeless women named Doris and Meg, then learning of two Loch Mallaig girls of the same name. Girls who would be the same age as Doris and Meg if they'd lived. But, of course, Doris had not.

Carol tapped her fingers on her steering wheel as she waited at a stop sign. She wondered about the specifics of how Doris Layville had died. It felt a little ghoulish to ask Kendra, but she could try to find out online. Harvey was often able to dig up the strangest information through Internet searches.

As she drove farther from downtown, the landscape became more filled with snow-covered trees. The many evergreens held thick snow in their strong arms. The brutal cold could sometimes make her forget the amazing beauty all around her. She slowed her car as she reached roads less traveled since she knew there could be ice.

She was glad of the reduction in speed when a deer emerged from the woods lining the road. Carol stepped carefully on the brakes, slowing down in case the deer decided to make an ill-advised dash across the road. But this deer acted smarter than many. It merely watched Carol pass with its deep, dark eyes, then stepped into the road once the car was safely by. "Good thinking," Carol said aloud. "Be safe."

The light was already fading by the time she got home. The combination of the trees and the early winter sunsets made the late afternoon feel even later. Smoke drifted lazily above the chimney at the log house. Harvey had a fire going in the fireplace.

She pulled up next to the house and had started for the door when she heard her name. She found Harvey near the chicken coop and waved. "How are the girls?" she asked, as they often called the chickens.

"Feisty," he said. "I'm giving them fresh bedding, and then I'll be in."

Carol waved again in reply before heading into the house and the prospect of hot cocoa. As she stirred the milk on the stove, she gazed toward the fireplace. She was torn between wanting to track down information on Doris Layville and wanting to sip cocoa beside the fire and forget about anything that was uncomfortable or sad.

By the time the hot chocolate was done, she'd decided on a compromise. She carried her laptop into the big front room, where huge windows gave the illusion of bringing the outdoors in. Thankfully the fireplace kept the room warm and cozy. She settled into one of two leather recliners that faced the fireplace and set her cocoa on the small table between them. Then she opened the laptop and began to search.

By the time she heard Harvey stamping snow off his boots at the doorway, her cocoa was nearly gone and so was her patience. She had exhausted all the ways she could think of to find information on Doris Layville or Doris Barnside. She supposed it was possible that the death notice had simply been too long ago since Doris had died when Kendra was barely more than a baby, and it was only in more recent years that newspapers had begun posting their stories online.

"You're wearing your annoyed-teacher look," Harvey said as he walked over to drop a kiss on her head. "Something from work or something on the computer? You haven't been reading political commentary again, have you?"

Carol laughed. "No, though I do think it's good to stay informed. I'm actually trying to track down a death notice." She explained what she'd learned from Hamish, Fergus, and Kendra.

About halfway through the explanation, Harvey settled into the other leather chair, totally absorbed in her words. "Quite a coincidence," he remarked when she finished.

"That's what I thought." She glared at the computer. "But this thing isn't helping at all."

"Why do you want to see a death notice?" Harvey asked. "Are you doubting that she died?"

"Not really," Carol hedged. "I mean, Kendra said she was a toddler, so if her mother ran away for some reason, her grandparents could have lied to avoid answering hard questions, but they do love Kendra. They're good people."

"From what Kendra says."

"Kendra *and* Fergus. Fergus said his father was fond of Daniel Layville. And most of the time, I admire Gordon MacGregor's insight."

"Well, pass that beast over to me." Harvey held out his hand for the laptop. "I'll see what I can do. I have access to a few databases still."

"I was hoping you'd say that."

She cheerfully gave him the laptop, then settled down to drink the rest of her cocoa while she watched the flames flicker in the fireplace. The combination of the warmth and hypnotizing dance of the flames helped calm her earlier irritation. She was pleasantly sleepy when Harvey finally growled at the computer.

"You couldn't find it either?" Carol asked.

"Not a death notice," he said. "I did find the record of Kendra's name change from Kendra Barnside to Kendra Layville when she was six. Nothing on her mother's death, though."

"Is that odd?"

"It is indeed. It was a couple decades ago, sure, but records don't disappear easily. Not if you know where to search. I haven't given up, mind you, but I'll have to think a while to see if I can tackle it from a different direction."

"Is it possible that she isn't dead?" Carol suggested.

"If she isn't, she must have a different name," he said. "It's hard these days for someone to live without leaving some kind of trail I can pick up. That makes me inclined to think she actually died. But why can't I find a record of it?"

Carol had no answer to that.

Harvey clearly didn't need one. "I did find some newspaper articles about Kendra, though. She was an impressive student, and is every bit as impressive a teacher. Did you know she won a teacher of the year award last year?"

Carol shook her head. "I'm sure I must have seen that in the paper, but she wasn't the twins' teacher last year, so it didn't register."

Then she remembered Harvey's promise. "You were going to try to get information out of the deputy chief while you gave your statement. I assume that didn't go well or you would have told me.

Did he not react to the names?"

"Oh, he reacted, all right," Harvey said firmly. "He didn't gasp or anything so obvious. He's good, but I've been a journalist for a long time. The names sharpened the man's expression, though he wouldn't comment on them at all."

"Did he ask where you'd come up with them?"

"Not as such. He did say he hoped the whole town wasn't gossiping about the case." He grinned at Carol. "I'm guessing he meant you."

"I should hope not," Carol said with a wounded sniff. "I do not gossip."

Harvey held up both hands. "I would never have agreed with him. At any rate, I have a question of my own. Have you spoken with Laura and Molly about the fishing trip yet?"

"Not yet," she said, changing the topic as quickly as she could. "I got a bit caught up in the idea of the bakehouse helping contribute a better quality of clothing to The Closet at St. Andrew's. Molly had some fantastic ideas."

"That's great," Harvey said. "Though I do hope you'll talk to them soon. Maybe tomorrow. I want us to go on the trip together. It'll be good for us both. I'm sure of it."

Carol hopped out of the chair. "I just remembered. I should have stopped at The Hamper for food on the way home. I'll have to go before we start supper. Be right back." She dropped a quick peck on Harvey's cheek and scampered for the door.

"I'll be here," he called after her.

Something in the way he said it told Carol that the fishing trip argument was far from over. She was going to have to deal with making a decision about her husband's inconvenient dream vacation—the sooner the better.

11

At The Hamper, Carol eased her car in between a battered pickup and a huge mound of snow, built up from several serious snowfalls that had been pushed aside by the town's plow. The small grocery didn't offer as many options as some of the huge places she'd shopped at in Pittsburgh, but in the summer, The Hamper was a wealth of local produce, which more than made up for the smaller selection in Carol's opinion.

She swung open her door and examined the pavement for ice before hopping out. She had no real plan for what to buy since her trip had been motivated by the desire to end the discussion about the fishing trip with Harvey. She could hardly believe he'd even brought it up in light of the death in the school parking lot. Didn't he know she couldn't possibly trundle off for a vacation in the middle of that?

As if Harvey were there with her, she could hear his voice in her head, calmly reminding her that the police in Loch Mallaig were perfectly capable of solving crimes without her help and had done it for years before she and her friends had moved there and opened the bakehouse.

"Sure," she muttered aloud as she stepped through the automatic doors into the store, "but that doesn't mean they don't need me now."

A young man passing her with a bag of groceries gave her a questioning appraisal.

She merely smiled at him and breezed by.

Though well-illuminated, the interior had an almost golden hue, making Carol assume they didn't use the same starkly white lights as in bigger stores. The warmer light made the store feel cozier, as did the slightly narrower aisles and the overall smaller footprint. Carol strolled to the rear of the store to see what the meat department had in stock. Maybe a nice steak would distract Harvey from more questions.

As if the universe had approved her decision, she found Greer Anderson pondering the selection of wrapped meat. Greer still wore her perfectly pressed police uniform. Her wavy blonde hair was pinned up in a neat bun, and she had one of the shop baskets looped over one arm. Greer was considerably shorter than Carol, but she carried herself with a confident posture that made her seem taller than she was.

Carol walked to the nearby case that held a selection of steaks and picked up a package, then she cut her eyes toward Greer. "You making last-minute supper choices too?"

Greer jumped, then grinned when she saw who'd spoken. "My sister is going vegan for the new year. She's been shaming me, so I cut back on buying meat. And now I have nothing at home I actually want to eat. I love my sister, but I can't imagine never buying another steak."

"I'm afraid Harvey would leave me if I tried cutting out meat entirely," Carol joked. "But it can be a healthy lifestyle choice."

Greer groaned. "So I've heard, over and over and over." She finally grabbed a package of meat and quickly dropped it in her basket as if hiding contraband.

"Greer?" Carol asked, knowing she was pushing her luck. "Was the victim found in the parking lot Doris or Meg?"

Greer quickly stepped closer to Carol and lowered her voice to a whisper. "How did you know about those two?"

"They've been hanging out at the library," Carol said. "Grizela told me about them. So which one of them did we find?"

With her voice still too low to carry beyond the two of them, Greer admitted, "It was Meg. Meg Shumway. She was in the system for minor offenses, shoplifting mostly."

"She didn't deserve to die."

"No, she didn't." Greer shook her head slowly. "But she wouldn't have lived much longer. She was riddled with cancer. The coroner said she must have been in a lot of pain."

"Cancer?" Carol repeated. "So she was sick. Did she trip and fall and hit her head on the dumpster?"

"Oliver doesn't think so," Greer said, referring to Oliver Fitzgerald, the local coroner and owner of the remaining funeral parlor in town. He was very competent, so any judgment he made was likely to be sound. "A blow to the head is what killed her, and Oliver found rust in the wound consistent with the dumpster, but he doesn't think it was from tripping and falling. There are a lot more tests pending, so we don't have a definitive ruling."

Carol digested this briefly, but she didn't let the moment stretch long. She didn't want Greer to get away while she was in a sharing mood. "Have you found her friend Doris yet?"

"Not yet. We've been hunting for her, but since we have no address or any idea where she's been staying, we don't know where else to search. Oliver said Meg hasn't been eating well and she was suffering from exposure too. Of course, the eating could have been from the cancer, but the exposure suggests they don't have stable housing."

"Or warm clothing," Carol replied.

"Maybe." The officer studied the contents of her basket, then locked eyes with Carol. "I know you're not a gossip, but don't say anything to anyone that suggests we see Doris as a possible suspect. We have no real reason to suspect her beyond her being Meg's friend, and I doubt she needs the extra stress of community censure. Right now, she's merely a person of interest. We want to ask her some questions, not arrest her."

"Good," Carol said. "You know, I did hear an interesting story about two past Loch Mallaig residents named Meg and Doris. They would be about the right age today." She explained about the wild girls, the cow incident, and how they'd moved out of town.

"Interesting," Greer said.

"But possibly irrelevant. Doris shares the same maiden name and ethnicity as a teacher at the grade school named Kendra Layville, but Kendra says her mother died when she was young. Harvey hasn't been able to track down a death notice, and he is brilliant at research. I believe it's worth examining further."

A sharp focus came into Greer's features, and Carol realized she had snapped into officer mode. "You said there were three of these girls. What was the third one's last name? Also, was the Meg in the story named Shumway?"

"I don't know the last names of Meg and Millie," Carol admitted. "Fergus remembered Doris's last name because her dad worked for Gordon MacGregor at Castleglen."

"But they all went to Loch Mallaig High School? I should be able to track down some information there. Thanks for bringing all this to my attention."

"It honestly might not be related," Carol admitted. "But the coincidence bothered me."

"Life is full of coincidences," Greer said. "But it's worth finding out if that's all this is."

Carol spotted a tiny woman in huge glasses heading her way at speed, her face almost glowing with excitement. "I think we're about to have company," she murmured.

Without a pause, Greer waved toward the other side of the store.

"Thanks for that tip on the produce. I'd better go see if they have the good salad mix in." She walked away from Carol as if they hadn't been in intense conversation moments before.

Carol offered a politely interested smile as the other woman reached her and began gushing about the melting moments cookies she'd bought at Bread on Arrival and taken to a holiday party. "Someone thought I'd made them," she said, her cheeks pinking. "And I should have disagreed, but I didn't. Do you think I could get the recipe for them?"

"It's not a trade secret," Carol said. "Come by the bakehouse. I'll write it out for you and leave it at the front counter."

The woman actually clapped her hands enthusiastically. "Thank you so much. I'll be in first thing tomorrow."

"Actually," Carol added on a whim, "I'll trade it for a warm sweater or coat donated to our clothing drive. If you have any to share, that is."

"I'd be delighted," the lady agreed. "I lost some weight last summer, so I have plenty to bring in."

"Wonderful. See you soon." Carol watched the woman rush away, her step positively springing. *It's nice to make someone happy that easily.* She supposed it was the magic of baked goods. They sweeten up life.

She peered down at the steaks she'd tossed into her basket without much thought. They were probably a little large. Maybe they didn't need that much red meat at one meal. She switched the package for one that was marginally smaller, then made her way toward produce for a couple of russet potatoes to bake.

After that, she picked up a package of butter she'd mix with herbs to baste the steaks, then headed for the checkout. The supper probably wouldn't distract Harvey from questions about the fishing trip, but it might at least give them both happy tummies, as Maisie and Gavin would say.

She'd nearly reached the single cashier when someone stepped out of the aisle ahead of her and blocked her way. "I'd love to give you a piece of my mind," Byron Quayle hissed.

Carol didn't reply, only examined him calmly. Though he was dressed differently from Officer Anderson, his clothing had the same feeling of crisp care, as if he'd never allow a wrinkle or a mess on it anywhere. How did a teacher possibly stay so neat, especially after a long day? Carol had always felt a bit limp and wrung out after a full day in the classroom.

"Well?" the man prompted.

"You said you wanted to talk to me," Carol replied. "You said nothing about me responding to you. And since your tone was quite rude, I thought it best not to answer."

He continued in the same manner. "I saw you going into the school today. I was on bus duty and couldn't say anything to you then. But I want to insist you halt any further involvement in this silly school 'mystery.' It's in the hands of the police now."

"And I assure you, the police will let me know if they have a problem with my actions."

Byron positively vibrated with annoyance. "Anything you and your cohorts do could get back to the principal. That could endanger the job of every teacher who has spoken to you, including me. Don't you care?"

Carol considered carefully what she should say next. His attitude pricked at her stubborn nature. She wasn't a fan of being ordered around by officious people. But if he was truly afraid for his job, perhaps she was being unfair.

A familiar voice said, "Byron."

Carol and Byron spun to face the elementary school principal. From the corner of her eye, Carol saw the teacher blanch.

"Hello, Mrs. Dour," Carol said pleasantly while the young teacher beside her stammered a rather muddled greeting of his own.

The principal gave her a bare glance, zeroing in on Byron. "Why are you telling Mrs. MacCallan that I'm going to fire you? Have you done something to warrant firing?"

He swallowed hard. "I merely wanted her to stop interfering in school business. I know that was upsetting you."

"I'll speak on my own behalf, thank you. You can go do your shopping."

The young man's color didn't improve, but he practically ran out of the store. If he'd come in to shop, he was leaving empty-handed.

"You must think me a monster," the principal said, her cool gaze on Carol.

"I don't necessarily think anything, but your employee's impression tells me a lot."

"I believe Byron Quayle thinks his future success depends on obsequiousness," Camilla said. "He should stand up to me the way Kendra does. I admire that far more. Although I was extremely upset at the idea of gossip stirring up parents."

"But there were break-ins at the school," Carol said firmly. "And someone has died. I can't see how you'll keep a lid on that."

The other woman's rigid posture slumped slightly. In an instant, she was transformed from the queen bee to a weary woman after a long day. "Yes, both of those things are true. And I'm willing to accept that I've overreacted all around."

"Oh?"

"Are you aware that I haven't been principal at the elementary school long?"

Carol nodded. She'd been friendly with the former principal, Bitsy Barkley, who had met the love of her life while on summer vacation and moved across the country to start fresh.

"I was the assistant principal at a middle school in a much larger city," Camilla went on. "Something happened, something that wasn't my fault or the principal's fault. Something that couldn't have been avoided. We run schools, not prisons. Young people who are determined to get into trouble often find a way."

"I was a teacher for many years," Carol said. "I know how much trouble a determined kid can get into."

"Well, the school board apparently didn't," the principal said. "They fired the principal as a scapegoat to end public criticism of the school. It wasn't fair or right. I quit in protest."

Carol raised her eyebrows, gaining new respect for this woman. "Good for you."

"Not so much. It took me the better part of a year to find another position. I was extremely fortunate to end up here in Loch Mallaig." She drew herself tall again and made the next statement sound like a painful confession. "As I said, I overreacted, and I've treated my teachers rather poorly. I intend to apologize to them all." She smiled a little, and suddenly she looked more human than Carol had ever seen her. "Even Byron."

"That's probably for the best," Carol said.

The principal continued to smile at her. "Any further questions?"

"Not at the moment, but I'm always asking questions."

"A good habit for a teacher. Though you have to be ready for the possibility it will get you into trouble."

"If it does, it won't be the first time."

"As long as it's not the last," the other woman said, then she bid Carol a good evening and strode away down the aisle, her spine ramrod straight.

Carol watched her go. The principal was a complicated person, but she wasn't nearly the dragon lady she had seemed.

Thoughts of the conversations she'd had at The Hamper followed Carol all the way home. When she pulled up at the house, another difficult discussion came to mind, and Carol suspected the fishing trip dilemma would still be waiting for her. It wasn't that she didn't want to go. She loved spending time with Harvey. If anything, they'd grown closer in retirement, unlike some couples she knew.

Stop being silly and sort this out! She grabbed the grocery bag from the seat beside her and hopped out of the car. When she slammed the door and started for the house, the sound disturbed the chickens. She could hear them protesting from the coop. In fact, the chickens were fussing enough that it made Carol wonder.

Carol changed direction and headed for the coop. Though it was barely suppertime, winter darkness had fallen. Some moonlight helped show the way to the coop, but deep shadows made everything a bit spooky. When Carol reached the coop and peeked inside, she found the chickens fine, if a little ruffled. There was no sign of a dog or a fox, the two main creatures they worried about with the hens once they were all cozy inside.

"What's got your feathers mussed?" she asked them.

The chickens had nothing to say on the subject. They simply watched her with their sharp, black eyes. She patted a couple and told them to settle down, that everything was fine. It wasn't until she'd started toward the house that she saw movement from the corner of her eye. A shadow had detached itself from a large tree near the edge of their yard.

A human-size shadow.

"Harvey?" Carol called, but the shadow didn't respond. Instead, it sank toward the deeper darkness of the woods beyond.

The cold around her suddenly felt much, much more threatening, and Carol crept toward the house. Something was out there. Something big enough to be a man or a bear.

The shadowy figure suddenly reversed direction and hurtled toward her.

"Harvey!" Carol screamed as she launched into a sprint for her life.

12

Harvey threw open the door and stepped out on the covered stoop. The light surrounded him in a welcome bit of refuge. "Carol?"

She practically plowed into him, but spun and pointed. "There's something in the tree line. It scared the chickens. It's big. A person, or maybe a bear."

Harvey edged past her and she let him go, though she wanted to pull him all the way into the house and lock them both inside. If she'd seen a bear, neither of them needed to get any closer to it.

To her relief, he walked to the bottom of the steps and a few yards down the path to the coop, then stopped. "I don't see anything."

"Whatever it was, it came this way with me in plain sight and calling out," Carol said. "I decided not to stick around. It had the girls all upset."

Harvey walked a few feet closer to the chicken coop, and Carol wondered if she shouldn't have mentioned them. Harvey might actually stand up to a bear to protect his beloved hens. "They are quiet now."

"I checked in on them," she said. "And they calmed down."

For a long moment Harvey stood there, peering into the darkness. "Whatever you saw must have moved into the woods," he finally said. "Let's get going on supper. I'm starving. Did you pick up anything interesting?"

Carol was more than happy to get inside and shut the door firmly behind them. She handed Harvey the bag as she shucked off her boots and coat. "Steak," she said. "I thought it would be a nice treat. We don't have it much in the winter."

"That's because no one wants to stand out in the cold and run the gas grill," he said. "Even for steak."

She nudged him with her shoulder. "No one is going to send you out in the cold. I've done enough of that for one night. We can pop them under the broiler."

In the kitchen, they got to work on the dinner preparations. Carol combined fresh basil, oregano, parsley, and rosemary she grew on a window shelf in the winter, then added garlic. Harvey scrubbed the potatoes and vented them thoroughly with a fork.

"Anything green?" he asked. "Or are we simply going to throw healthy eating to the wind?"

"I have peas in the freezer." Carol unwrapped a stick of butter and set it on a plate to soften in the microwave. "Do you think that could have been a bear I saw?"

He shook his head as he slid the potatoes into the oven. "It's not impossible, but highly unlikely. All our bears are sound asleep these days. Maybe it was Bigfoot."

"The only big feet around here are yours."

Harvey laughed. "I imagine you saw a neighbor or a bird-watcher in the woods. With the leaves off the trees, someone could be out looking for owls. It could even have been Hamish. He was quite interested when I told him about our owl population on Sunday after church."

Carol shook her head. "Hamish would have answered when I called out."

"Maybe he did," Harvey said as he closed the oven door. "The wind was at your back since it comes off the lake. It would have made it easy for him to hear you but hard for you to hear him. You said the figure started toward you. Maybe it was someone we know, but when you sprinted off like a gazelle, the person returned to owl hunting."

Carol rolled her eyes. "My sprinting-gazelle days are long over."

He leaned over and kissed her cheek. "You'll always be a gazelle to me." He winked at her when she laughed. "At the risk of changing the subject, I'm going to go over to the library tomorrow morning. I can track down the high school yearbooks from back in Fergus's day. Maybe I can find out the last names of our Wild'uns."

Carol paused in combining the butter and herbs. "Do you think Meg could have been one of those girls? If Doris Layville is dead, she can't be the Doris who has been with our Meg at the library."

"It's worth checking out. First, we know Kendra *said* Doris is dead, but death doesn't go unremarked in a loving family. I am deeply bothered that I couldn't find a death notice."

"Sometimes records do get lost," Carol said.

"Okay, suppose Doris Layville is dead. It's possible Millie is going by Doris's name."

"That sounds pretty far-fetched. Why would she do that?"

"I don't know, but I've uncovered more far-fetched stories in my career that were proven to be true." He leaned over the bowl of herb butter and gave a deep sniff. "That smells amazing."

"I love the scent of fresh herbs and garlic." She began shaping the herb butter into a disk before popping it in the refrigerator to firm up a little. "I ran into some folks at The Hamper."

"Oh?" Harvey asked with his head in the freezer, where he was digging around for the peas.

"First, I chatted with Greer Anderson at the meat case. She said the Meg we found has been identified as Meg Shumway, so if the Meg in the yearbooks is Meg Shumway, we'll know we're dealing with the Wild'uns."

"Unless the Meg we found got married and changed her last name."

"Right. Greer also said the Meg we found had cancer, late stage. She wouldn't have lived much longer."

Harvey winced. "Poor woman should have been in hospice, not lying behind a dumpster on a cold night."

"I broached the possibility that she'd fallen and hit her head on the dumpster. If she was that sick, she could have been unsteady on her feet."

"Solid theory," Harvey said.

"Greer told me they wouldn't totally rule that out, but Oliver said it would be extremely unlikely to create the wound they found. They think she was struck."

"Who would attack a dying woman?" Harvey asked. "She must have been rather feeble."

"A monster." Carol joined Harvey at the refrigerator, nudging him aside so she could put the butter in. "I also ran into one of the schoolteachers, Byron Quayle, and the principal. Those were interesting."

"Oh?" Harvey reached over her head and grabbed a bag of asparagus from the freezer. "Not peas."

"Peas are good."

"They make good ice bags for bruises," he said agreeably. "But asparagus makes a better complement for steak. What did the teacher and principal say?"

"The teacher acted as he has all along, but the principal was interesting. She apologized for being such a shrew in the past."

"Do tell."

"Apparently she worked with a principal who lost a job over something that couldn't have been prevented, and it's made her anxious. I suppose she worries about the same thing happening to her."

"What exactly happened to this other principal?"

"Mrs. Dour was light on the specifics, but she implied it had to do with a student's actions. She said she worked in a bigger city."

"What city?"

Carol shrugged. "As I said, she was light on specifics."

"Hmmm." Harvey laid the asparagus on the counter, his expression thoughtful. "That sounds like another angle I want more information on. I'll see what I can dig up."

She patted him gently on the cheek. "That's my ace reporter."

Throughout the preparation and all the way through eating the delicious supper, they kept up the kind of banter Carol loved. In many ways, it reminded her constantly of how grateful she was to be spending her life with Harvey. He was smart and made her laugh. And she knew, without question, that he loved her. She wished every couple could have such a relationship.

As with all meals, the eating didn't take nearly as long as the preparation, and soon Carol found herself wrist deep in hot water while Harvey dried the dishes beside her. They had a dishwasher, but Carol sometimes favored washing the dishes by hand, especially when it would extend their time together.

They'd run out of topics to chat about, but Carol didn't mind. At least Harvey hadn't brought up the fishing trip. She scrubbed the broiler pan while listening to Harvey hum under his breath. Harvey didn't have a bad singing voice, but his humming could be questionable and sometimes a bit aimless. "Is that a hymn you're singing?" she asked.

"You can't tell?" he asked as he wiped the last dish and put it in the cupboard. "It was 'Rock of Ages.' I thought that was one of your favorites."

"It is," she said. "I probably wasn't listening closely."

"Must not have been."

At the ringing of the phone, Carol took the chance to escape possible ridicule for not following her husband's erratic humming. She called to Harvey as she hurried from the kitchen, "The broiler pan is clean. Rinse it for me, please?" She snagged the landline in the living room area. "Hello?"

"Mom, what are you up to now?"

"Hello, Jenny," Carol said, choosing to ignore her daughter's accusatory tone. "How are you? How are the twins?"

"The twins are full of stories," she said. "They brought them home from school. All about how Grandma is on a murder case."

"What?" *How did the children at the school find out about the body?* The answer came to her at once. Adults often thought children paid their conversations no mind—but when it came to juicy gossip, children were often listening. One of the staff merely needed to mention it in front of one child and the word would spread. Carol could have smacked herself. She should have expected this.

"So you're not on a case?" Jenny asked, her tone far too mild. "The children seem to think you're part of a murder investigation."

Carol was tempted to make a joke about the imaginations of children, but she didn't want to lie to Jenny, not even by omission or misdirection. "It appears that the woman we found behind the dumpster was killed," Carol said. "The poor thing had been living rough, and Greer told me she had cancer."

"That's so sad," Jenny said, echoing Carol and Harvey's thoughts about it. "So you and the gang are trying to find out what happened to her?"

Something about the way Jenny said "the gang" made Carol realize something she hadn't even considered. She had hurt Jenny's feelings somehow. "Jenny, are you upset because we didn't bring you along?"

Jenny scoffed. "I couldn't have come. I have two small children, remember?"

"As if Craig couldn't have put Maisie and Gavin to bed."

"Well, yes, sure, he would and does. But still. I don't mind that I wasn't there." She paused for a moment and Carol heard her take a deep breath. "Mom, what hurts my feelings is that you didn't tell me.

We were with you on Sunday, and you didn't even bring it up. We're talking about the school that Maisie and Gavin attend. Don't you think I should have been told sooner how serious it is?"

"In retrospect, yes," Carol admitted. "In fact, I wondered if perhaps the twins should take some time off."

"I don't think we need to go that far. And don't think you're the only one to get an earful from me. I called Kendra too. She may not be so quick to call on my mother, the sleuth, in the future."

"Honey, don't blame Kendra. I don't think she was happy about the idea either. And she was dealing with a lot of blowback from another teacher who didn't want word to get around."

"Fine," Jenny said. "I know that schools can be more of a soap opera than anything on television. But I'm still not happy. You should have told me."

"You're right. I should have. I'm so sorry. I wouldn't hurt your feelings for the world. I suppose I was partially motivated by not wanting you to worry."

"That's the thing, Mom. I worry so much more when I know you'll keep things from me. It means I never know when you could be doing something crazy."

"Your father does his best to keep me on an even keel."

"He doesn't stand a chance."

"Well, there's that." Carol paused. "Listen, do you want to be involved now?"

"Yes, Mom. I do."

"Great," Carol said, pushing extra enthusiasm into the word. "Your father is going over to the library in the morning as soon as it opens. He wants to look up some information in old high school yearbooks. You can join him, if you're free. I don't know if that fits your class schedule."

"I'm available," Jenny said decisively. "My classes start later in the day, and I can take a sick day if necessary."

"I don't imagine you'll need a sick day," Carol said. "But if you have a free morning, I know your dad would enjoy your company."

"I always love Jenny's company," Harvey hollered from the kitchen, scaring Pascal, who was tiptoeing out of their bedroom. The skittish cat vanished again.

"Good, then I'll meet him in front of the library," Jenny said. Carol heard voices shouting in the background. Jenny's voice held a mixture of amusement and annoyance when she spoke again. "Mom, I have to go. There's a bath-time catastrophe involving a tsunami."

"Bye, honey. Kiss the kids for me."

When the call ended, Carol knew she'd been forgiven, or at least mostly. Jenny had sounded enthusiastic about joining her father in the morning.

"Jenny is excited about being your partner in sleuthing tomorrow," she said as she walked to the kitchen.

Harvey was neatly hanging the damp towel to dry. "Lucky me. We don't get to spend enough time together. Is she mad at you?"

"Some. I'm afraid I've been treating her like a child by keeping her out of this," Carol said. "I've been trying to protect her from worry and making her worry all the more. I'm turning over a new leaf."

"Good for you." He threw an arm around her. "Want to watch some television? I recorded one of those British mysteries you enjoy so much."

Carol leaned into the hug. "That sounds absolutely wonderful. I'll grab my knitting while we watch. I can try to finish that sweater to donate to the church."

"I'd call that a plan. You go get your knitting, and I'll fix popcorn."

"We just ate."

"I always have room for popcorn."

With a chuckle, Carol headed off to the bedroom to get her knitting bag and maybe apologize to Pascal for his scare. May as well get all her apologizing done in one night.

When she reached the bedroom, she found the cat curled up on the bed, asleep. Since he spent most of his time under it, she decided not to disturb him. As she got her knitting bag from the side table next to the bed, she glanced toward the window that faced the chicken coop. In the distance, she could barely make out the stand of trees, which reminded her of her earlier scare.

Had she really seen a neighbor or a bird-watcher? With a shrug, she realized she'd probably never know. It wasn't as if it mattered.

Did it?

13

Carol pulled up to Bread on Arrival on Tuesday morning with renewed cheer. It didn't hurt that temperatures had risen overnight and the weather report promised a sunny day. Not that the sun had made much of an appearance yet. Baker's hours didn't let Carol see a lot of sunrises for most of the year, but she didn't mind. She couldn't think of a better way to start the day than surrounded by friends and the pleasure of baking.

She'd barely gotten inside and suspected she might be the first one to arrive when she heard the clatter of footsteps on the stairs to the second floor. "Hi Carol," Molly called. "I saw you pull in. Come upstairs to the office. I have something to show you."

"Be right there," Carol sang out. "Let me take off my coat."

When she reached the top of the stairs, she found Angus dancing around with joy at her arrival. She bent to pet the little dog. "What's your human up to?" Carol asked Angus quietly, but if the little dog had an answer other than making sure she had enough doggy kisses, he wasn't sharing.

Most of the second floor of the bakehouse was taken up by Molly's apartment, but there was also a storage room and the large bakery office with its accompanying closet. The office had a door to an exterior staircase that led down to Angus's fenced area, which they playfully called his barking lot. Though Angus didn't always feel stalwart enough to brave the cold, Carol suspected the warm afternoon would entice him out.

Molly sat at the office desk, staring at the screen. When Carol came in, Molly waved her over. "Come and check this out," she said. "This is the ad I'm going to put in the *Crown Press News.*"

Carol leaned over to see what Molly had made. The ad featured cute images of winter coats and steaming mugs, along with a large print caption: *Sweet Gifting: Warmth for Warmth!* The smaller print underneath promised a free hot beverage or cookie for anyone bringing in gently used coats and sweaters for adults.

"That's terrific," Carol said. "Laura's going to love it too."

"I've made signs for the shop and I've printed handbills. I'm going to get Bridget and some of her college friends to help distribute them," Molly explained.

Bridget Ross helped out at the bakehouse in between taking forensic science classes at Superior Bay College. She was vital to staying on top of the summer crowds, though she worked fewer hours in the winter. Carol suspected she wouldn't mind a few more dollars. She'd rarely met a college student who didn't need a little extra cash.

"I'm so impressed," Carol said.

Molly beamed at her. "I'm glad you brought it up. I love this kind of thing." She pulled one sign out of the pile. "Fergus promised to put up a sign at Castleglen, so I figured one of us could run this over to him later."

Carol grinned at her friend. "One of us?"

"Don't tease. You and Laura both enjoy seeing me blush too much. I'd hoped the teasing would stop now that Fergus and I are actually dating."

"Molly, I love you like a sister, but it's time to face facts," Carol told her. "The teasing will *never* stop. But I promise to try to keep it down to a tolerable level."

"Gee, thanks," Molly said, then hopped out of the chair. "We should get downstairs to work."

"I have things to tell you and Laura," Carol said. "But I'll hold off until she gets here so I only have to say them once."

"You're making me wait?" Molly pulled a face. "That's almost worse than teasing."

Carol chuckled as she stooped to give Angus a little more affection before heading downstairs.

"He'll nap for a while now," Molly said. "I took him out when we first got up, and we ran around in the snow at the park."

"Sounds chilly."

"Not if you bundle up like a bear," Molly said.

Her words reminded Carol again of the figure she'd seen near the woods. She made a mental note to ask Hamish if it was a good time for owl spotting. They reached the bottom of the stairs in time to hear the back door open. Laura had arrived, so their day could officially begin.

Laura and Molly jumped on the morning bread orders, with Molly mostly measuring ingredients into mixing bowls. The bread order was always big. Many local restaurants exclusively used bread from the bakehouse, and more than a few bought desserts from Bread on Arrival as well. In addition to bread, they produced virtually all the desserts for Castleglen, which was a big order all by itself, even in the winter. Carol was always amazed that the resort even stayed open in winter since no one would be golfing, but Fergus consistently had guests all year round. The town's other golf venue, Moose Lake Country Club, closed for the icy months. She knew, though, that some people actually preferred the quieter months at Castleglen, and it remained quite popular for social events and business retreats as well. With the great restaurants and the spa, they did more than enough business to warrant staying open.

While her friends were making loaves and buns, Carol concentrated on the breakfast offerings, mostly bagels and scones, which were always hugely popular.

"Carol, are you ever going to tell us about the news you hinted at upstairs?" Molly asked a while later.

Carol was rolling out dough for blueberry scones. "Oh, right." She neatened the circle of dough as she launched into a recounting of her chat with Greer and her conversations with the principal and Byron Quayle. Her friends listened raptly as she talked.

"So do you believe the principal?" Laura asked as she cut dough to pop into bread pans. "That she overreacted because of some other incident at another school?"

"I don't know," Carol admitted. "Probably. She sounded sincere."

"Shall I name the many people we've met who have sounded sincere but were hiding secrets?" Laura asked. "Would you like the list chronologically or alphabetically?"

"You're a touch cynical," Carol observed as she cut the dough into portions.

Laura dusted flour from her hands and shook her head. "I'm realistic. Still, if you believe she was sincere, I'll give her a tentative pass. What about the teacher?"

"I think he is genuinely worried about his job," Carol said as she remembered the man's pale face. "He's also obnoxious, though I'm not sure that's enough reason to think he's a suspect."

"Probably not," Laura said. "Now, on a different note, Hamish is coming in late today so one of us will need to open. I haven't taken a turn in a while. Do you want me to do it?"

"I can do it," Molly offered quickly. "I'm always more secure when you are baking. I'm sort of the weak link."

Carol began moving the scones to a pan for baking. "That's not true. And today, I'd like to open, if it's okay with both of you. Harvey and Jenny are going over to the library this morning to look through some yearbooks. I figure they might come in for coffee and breakfast. Since Jenny has been a bit miffed at me, I want to be up front if that happens."

"Fair enough," Molly said. "Daughters always come first." Molly's own daughter, Chloe, was a veterinarian in Milwaukee and lived too far away to drop in easily. Molly missed her badly sometimes.

Once the scones were in the oven, Carol glanced at the clock. "I have time to get a batch of bannock made before I need to go up front to make sure everything's ready." She began to gather ingredients. "I really hope Harvey and Jenny are able to find a conclusive answer about whether the Doris and Meg of Fergus's story are the same women who hung out at the library."

"Even if he finds them in the yearbook, I'm not sure that would settle anything," Laura said. "We know they went to school in Loch Mallaig."

"We do, but remember, Greer told me the Meg who died is Meg Shumway. If Meg never married, she'll be Meg Shumway in the yearbook," Carol said.

"That's a big if," Molly said. "How many women never marry?"

"Hey, I never married," Laura said. "That makes one out of three right here."

If one out of three of the Loch Mallaig High wild girls had never married, Carol hoped the one was Meg. Then they'd finally have some forward momentum on finding out what was going on.

Finally, all the morning breakfast goods were done and the air was filled with the scent of fresh scones and baking bread. Carol carried a pan of scones to the front and began filling the case. She'd made both blueberry and chocolate-cherry, using berries frozen the previous summer. For those who favored a savory scone, she'd made the herb and cheese version that was always a hit.

Sometimes she worried that having such a wide variety of scones during the slowest of the winter months wasn't a good idea, but they rarely had leftovers. Loch Mallaig had plenty of die-hard scone lovers, and the Empire biscuits with their luscious jam fillings were usually a sellout as well. Carol inventoried all the cookies, making note of the ones that they'd need to bake first. Cookies didn't start selling big until afternoon, so they came after breads in the morning priorities.

When she finally flipped the sign from *Closed* to *Open*, Carol peered out at the street, hoping to see Harvey and Jenny, but they weren't there. Of course, it was only seven. The library wouldn't open for another two hours.

As it happened, Harvey and Jenny didn't come in before the library opened, though a steady stream of customers kept Carol too busy to think about it much.

When the rush of customers hungry for breakfast ebbed, Carol had a chance to check the time. Hamish would be in soon to take over for her. Harvey and Jenny must not be coming by.

She fought down her disappointment and reminded herself that at least Jenny wouldn't feel so left out now.

Right on time, Hamish walked up behind her, grumbling about the weather. "What's wrong?" Carol asked. "We're supposed to have a beautiful day."

He harrumphed. "The sun was in my eyes all the way down my driveway. It's enough to blind a man."

Carol chuckled. Hamish could find something to complain about in paradise. "Hamish, I have a question for you."

Suspicion crept into his features. "Does it involve my coming in early?"

"No, nothing like that."

"Too bad. Joyce is working me to death in the mornings lately."

Carol thought Hamish looked perfectly hale and hearty to her, but she decided not to comment on it. "I was wondering, would this be a good time of year to spot owls at night?"

"That's an interesting question. Snowy owls tend to migrate to our fair state for the winter, and they're gorgeous creatures. With all the trees bare of leaves, owls are easier to see, but bird-watching at night in January is a little dangerous with the cold. Hypothermia can sneak up on a person."

"So you wouldn't expect to see anyone out hunting for owls?"

He flinched. "I prefer not to use the word 'hunting' when discussing bird-watching. Also, I expect people to do crazy things all year round. And I do search for owls around our house at night, though I don't head deep in the woods much after dark."

So Harvey could have been right. Well, not about Bigfoot, but about someone out searching for owls. "Thanks, Hamish."

Hamish moved away to respond to a man who'd approached the counter for a coffee refill. The bell over the door gave its cheerful jingle, and Carol was delighted to see Harvey hold the door open so Jenny could walk in, holding a small pile of books that Carol assumed were yearbooks from the high school.

Carol walked around the counter to join them. "Are those the yearbooks?" she asked. "How did you get them? Grizela doesn't usually let them out of the building."

"I believe Dad could charm the stars out of the sky," Jenny said with a giggle. "It's always a treat to see him in action."

"I had to promise Grizela that I'd guard them with my life," Harvey said. "But I think she feels sorry for any book that doesn't get much attention, even if they're yearbooks."

"A true librarian," Carol said. "Did you find anything in them?"

Harvey shook his head. "We haven't gone through them yet. You can help if the bakehouse can spare you."

Carol glanced toward Hamish. She didn't doubt that he'd been eavesdropping and, sure enough, he nodded.

"I believe I can," Carol said cheerily. "Can I get you a scone and some coffee?"

"That would be heavenly," Jenny said. "Though would you mind making it to go for me? I need to head to the school." She handed the pile of books to her father, who carried them to an empty table.

"Blueberry scone?" Carol asked, knowing her daughter preferred sweet over savory. "Or chocolate-cherry?"

"You need to ask?" Jenny said as she sank into a chair across from her dad. "Chocolate, of course."

"Coming right up."

When Carol returned with hot drinks and scones, Jenny stood up and accepted her coffee and scone from her mother. "Thanks, Mom. I'm going to run, but text me if you discover anything interesting. Thank you both. This was fun."

"Thank you for helping," Carol said.

"And for not laughing at me while I was trying to charm Grizela," Harvey said.

"That was the hard part." Jenny gave them each a hug and left.

Harvey slid a yearbook to Carol as she sat in the chair Jenny had vacated. As she flipped through the book from back to front, she was amused to see she recognized many of the names of the students, who were now middle-aged bakehouse patrons. Suddenly she stopped and gawked at a photo. The photo showed a teenager who bore a startling resemblance to Kendra Layville.

"Wow, Kendra is a perfect replica of her mom," Carol said as she spun the book to show him the photo of Doris Layville.

"I believe you found the first Wild'un," Harvey said. "One down, two to go."

Carol stared into Doris Layville's eyes for another moment. She beamed with happiness in the photo, and Carol thought sadly that she should have had a long, happy life ahead of her, but that life had purportedly been snuffed out a few short years after this photo had been taken.

She continued flipping through the photo section and quickly found a Meg Shumway. Though Carol had only the briefest glimpse of the dead woman, she saw nothing of that worn face in this photo. The girl in the picture was full of hope and mischief.

"I found Meg Shumway," Carol said, her voice subdued. "Since the Meg here has the same name as the Meg in the parking lot, it's likely she was still with the same Doris she hung out with in high school."

"For them to be two different people is one coincidence too far," Harvey agreed.

"And that means Kendra's mother didn't die," Carol replied. "Why would Doris's parents have said she did?"

"I'd like to ask them." Harvey tapped the book. "See if you can find Millie."

Carol flipped through the pages slowly. She found no girls named Millie. "Could she have been in a different grade?" she asked.

"It's possible, though not probable," Harvey replied. "Remember high school. How many of your close friends were in different grade levels?"

"None. It wasn't until college that I made friends in different years." And she was glad she had, since she'd started Bread on Arrival with two of them.

"Maybe Millie was a nickname," Harvey suggested. "Check for a Millicent or an Amelia."

After another short bit of flipping, Carol reported, "No Amelia, but I did find a Millicent Dennison." She pointed to the photo of a girl in braces.

Harvey shrugged. "Could be. Hey, you can ask Hamish."

At the sound of his name, Hamish stood from where he'd been checking the trays in the display during a break in customer traffic. "Ask me what?"

"Could you come and look at this photo, please?" Carol asked.

Hamish obliged. "Looks like a teenager."

"Was this Millie?" Carol asked. "The wild girl from your stories."

"Oh." Hamish leaned over and studied the photo more closely. "It's been a lot of years, but I don't think so. Maybe? I don't remember her having braces. And I'm fairly sure her hair was darker, but I don't know."

"We have one other witness," Harvey said. "We should take the book to Castleglen and ask Fergus." Then he grinned. "And maybe get some lunch."

"You just had breakfast," Carol scolded. But she had to admit, the idea had appeal. Fergus may have a clearer memory of the girls. "Let me see if I can get away."

She went to the kitchen to tell Laura and Molly about their discovery and the possible next step in the process. Once again, she felt a thrill. They were finally on the right track—she was sure of it. Meg Shumway had been one of the Wild'uns and had died in the parking lot of the elementary school on Saturday night. Doris Layville had been Meg's close friend, and she was in Loch Mallaig as well, despite what Kendra had said and despite the fact that the police hadn't located her yet. Now they might be on the verge of discovering the third girl as well.

Carol wasn't sure whether Millie would end up being important, but she didn't doubt at all that Kendra was. The story of Doris's death was a mystery in itself, but they'd find the answer. She was sure of it.

14

Both Laura and Molly agreed immediately that Carol and Harvey should head over to Castleglen. "I'm free to take over the front for a bit," Molly said, "but let me run up and get the sign for Castleglen. You can give it to Fergus."

Carol felt a pang of guilt. The whole warm clothing drive had been Molly's idea, and she'd already forgotten about her friend's hard work. "Thanks, Molly," she said. "For everything. Sometime soon, we'll make sure you get some time off for a nice lunch with Fergus."

Molly simply beamed before dashing for the stairs. Carol pulled out her phone to call Fergus.

"Good morning, Carol," he said in greeting. "What can I do for one of my three favorite bakers?"

"I'm not sure that favoritism is evenly spread," Carol replied.

He chuckled. "Afraid not. I am especially partial to a certain blonde lady."

"She'll be glad to hear that. Actually, I wanted to ask you something related to the group of girls we talked about—Millie, Meg, and Doris."

"What do you want to know?"

"Was Millie's real name Millicent Dennison?"

"I have no idea," Fergus said. "I didn't hang out with those girls. I saw them around and heard gossip. You know how high schools are. The gossip buzzes like a beehive."

"Do you think you'd recognize a photo of her?" Carol asked.

"A photo of her today?" Fergus laughed. "I imagine her appearance has changed a lot over the years. I know mine has."

"No, a photo from high school," Carol said. "Harvey picked up some yearbooks from the library and we found photos of Doris and Meg, but we're not sure if Millicent Dennison is the Millie who ran around with them. If we came to Castleglen, could you spare a minute to flip through the pages of the yearbook and weigh in?"

"Sure," Fergus said. "We can meet at Tee for Two and have a comfortable conversation."

"That sounds great," Carol said. Tee for Two was a charming breakfast and lunch bistro in Castleglen's main lodge. The restaurant had extensive seating on the terrace, none of which would be in use in January, of course. The thought alone was enough to make Carol shiver. Although limited, the seating inside should be more than enough for the winter traffic, even though it was a popular spot with Loch Mallaig residents too. "Can we come right over?"

"As soon as you wish," Fergus said. "Give me a ring when you're close, and I'll meet you at the lodge entrance. You don't want to have to try to track me down. I'm all over the place this time of year."

True to his word, Fergus met Carol and Harvey as they entered the lodge. Though morning sun poured through the main windows in the front wall of the lodge's entry, the double-paned glass resisted the winter cold. The lodge was warm and inviting, including a snapping fire in one of the oversize fireplaces of the expansive lobby.

"What's that?" Fergus asked, gesturing to the sign Carol carried.

She handed it over. "A gift from Molly. I bet she was up late making it."

"No doubt," he agreed. "She's excited about this clothing drive. Which reminds me, I want to pitch in as well. I have some nice coats, and I'd like to donate some money. Maybe Molly could buy some new items for the drive? She has great taste."

"She certainly does," Carol agreed. *In boyfriends as well as clothes.*

As they walked through the large lodge foyer, several people greeted Fergus warmly, and he always paused for a moment to respond. Carol was impressed by the way he was able to make each person feel special and heard without falling into endless delays. Only once did he pause a bit longer, and that was to hand over Molly's sign and ask the staffer to take it to his office. "I'll post it as soon as you guys give me the signal," he told Carol.

"I never doubted it," Carol assured him.

When they reached Tee for Two, Fergus led the way to a table in a quiet corner. As soon as they were seated, Harvey handed over the yearbook. "I marked the page for Millicent Dennison."

"Thanks." Fergus scanned a few pages on the way to the marker. "I haven't opened my yearbook in ages. We were all so young."

"You were," Harvey said. "I know I was. A kid who thought he was an adult. And the haircuts." He shook his head.

"Have I seen your high school yearbook photo?" Carol asked him. "I honestly don't remember."

"You haven't," he said. "And you never will. Put it out of your mind."

Not possible, but that's a mystery for another occasion. Carol leaned forward in her seat slightly as Fergus reached the page with Millicent Dennison's photo. He stared at the teenager without speaking for several long moments. "That's not Millie," he said at last. "She is familiar, though. I saw her at one of the reunions. At any rate, she goes by Penny. I remember because she made it sound like a joke, though I didn't get it. I suppose I would have if I'd realized her name was Milli*cent*. The Millie I remember had darker hair anyway."

"That's what Hamish said." Carol groaned. "Maybe Millie didn't get her photo taken. People do get left out of yearbooks sometimes." She tapped the page. "That is the only Millicent, and there's no Amelia."

Fergus slowly flipped through the pages, his expression distracted. "I still know some of these people, of course. But we've all gotten old."

"Not old," Harvey said. "Just mature."

"I suppose." Suddenly Fergus sat up sharply and poked the page with his finger. "That's her. That's Millie."

Carol and Harvey leaned forward so sharply they nearly knocked heads. The young girl on the page did have dark hair and dark eyes, staring at them from behind thick glasses. She also had a startlingly large nose. No wonder Fergus could pick her out. This girl's features were distinctive.

Carol strained to read the small print under the name, but she couldn't, not upside down. "What is her name?"

"Camilla Fordyce," Fergus said.

"Millie was short for Camilla," Carol replied. "We hadn't considered that." She snapped her fingers. "Camilla is the first name of the principal at the elementary school, Camilla Dour."

Harvey tapped the page. "That is not her. Granted, I haven't seen the principal as much as you have, but she doesn't look like that *at all*. That's got to be a real coincidence."

"I suppose." Carol sat back in the chair. "So we know the three wild girls were Camilla Fordyce, Doris Layville, and Meg Shumway. Meg is the woman we found dead."

"Is she in here?" Fergus asked, flipping pages until he reached hers. "I remember Meg now. The woman in the parking lot was so different from the girl I knew."

"She seems to have had a hard life," Carol said. "And she was very sick."

"That's terrible." Fergus idly flipped more pages, barely glancing at them now. He finally stopped when a server came over and set coffee on the table for each of them. "I went ahead and preordered coffee, but if you guys are hungry, ask for anything. It's on the house."

"No, I'm fine," Carol said at nearly the same moment that Harvey asked for a menu. She gave him the look she'd perfected in the classroom for wayward students, but he ignored it.

As soon as Harvey had chosen a hearty breakfast, the server left and Fergus asked, "What have we gained by knowing the names of these girls?"

"I'm not sure. We know Doris Layville Barnside is still alive," Carol said. "Or we suspect it at the very least. Harvey is going to see if Grizela can confirm that the photo in the yearbook is the woman Grizela saw in the library. Other than that, I don't know."

"If the years have been as hard on her as they apparently were on Meg, that would be tough," Fergus said.

"I'm going to do more digging," Harvey said. "Now that we have strong reason to doubt Doris's death, I do have some semiofficial sources I can tap. It doesn't pay to call in too many favors unless it's important, but in this case, it is."

"How about her family? Are her parents still alive?" Fergus smiled. "I'd love to chat with Daniel Layville. I remember him so fondly. I could track down a number and call them, if you want."

"Dragging up talk about a dead child would be painful," Carol said. "And if she's not dead, and this is a secret they've been keeping, it could be even harder. Let's see if we can be sure with the Grizela angle first."

"Sounds reasonable. I'll hold on until I get the word. I'm always available." Fergus returned to flipping through the pages of the yearbook, then hooted with laughter.

"What?" Carol asked.

His cheeks pink, Fergus spun the book around to show a photo of himself.

Harvey burst out laughing. "You make me feel a lot better about my yearbook photo."

Carol gawked at it. "Wow, that's a lot of hair."

"I was heavily influenced by teen idols," Fergus admitted sheepishly.

Carol chuckled, but her eye was drawn further down the page to a photo she recognized. The years hadn't done too much to this boy. His face had sharper plains and he didn't have as much hair, but he was easily recognizable. "That man was the emergency tech who told us Meg had been dead for hours."

"That's Ballard Maddox, all right. He was such a big deal that year in high school, our star football player." Fergus's expression grew sad. "If I'm not mistaken, he lost a chance at a huge scholarship because of that cow prank, or because of the aftermath of it, anyway. I remember talk about it. It was a shame. He was a gifted athlete. He is obviously doing all right now, though."

"Helping people at their worst," Harvey said. "It's noble work."

"And hard," Fergus agreed.

With an effort, they shifted the conversation to cheerier subjects. Carol thanked Fergus for his help with the clothing drive. Again, he radiated pride over how hard Molly was working on the promotion, and that carried them through until Harvey's breakfast arrived.

When they finally left Castleglen, Harvey held open the car door for Carol with a deep bow. "Where shall I take thee, milady? Bread on Arrival? Or will you play hooky a little longer and go to the library with me?"

"The library," Carol said. "Otherwise, I'll only be distracted by curiosity waiting to hear from you."

"The library it is."

They arrived at the library a short while later. Harvey asked for Grizela at the circulation desk while Carol held the yearbooks and walked over to the comfortable chairs that Grizela had said were Doris's favorite reading spot. Though several of the chairs were filled by patrons reading, none wore the layers of clothing that would help identify them as Doris.

Grizela actually found Carol instead of the other way around. "Is that one of the yearbooks I loaned your husband?" she asked. "I hope you've been careful with them."

"We have," Carol promised. "But I did want to ask you a question about this one." She opened the book and pointed at Doris Layville's photo. "Is this the Doris who came in with Meg?"

Grizela harrumphed. "That's a child."

"I realize that, but this is also a yearbook from several decades ago. She's no longer a child. Can you tell if this girl grew up to be the Doris who came in with Meg?"

Grizela took the book from Carol, handling it as gingerly as if it were one of the fragile books in the genealogy room. She lifted a pair of glasses on a chain and set them on her nose to peer closely at the photo.

While Grizela was studying the image, Harvey joined them. "Leave it to you to find her first," he whispered to Carol.

Grizela finally pulled herself away from the page. "I can't say with complete certainty. A good many years have passed."

"All we want is your best guess," Carol said.

"I don't much care for guessing," Grizela grumbled. "As I said, I cannot be certain, but I do see some resemblance. And now that I'm seeing this photo, the Doris who came in here did remind me of someone else."

"Oh?" Carol asked.

"A teacher from the elementary school," Grizela explained. "The teachers come in regularly to pick up boxes of books for their classes. One of them bears a resemblance to the woman who came in here." She closed the yearbook. "So are you done with this? I should return it to the collection. Along with those." She indicated the other yearbooks, and Carol handed them over. "Now, if you don't have anything else to hold me up, I need to get to work. I've little time for dillydallying."

"And I need to get to the bakehouse," Carol said.

"I should think so." Grizela spun on her heel and marched away.

Once she was out of earshot, Harvey gave in to the chuckles he'd been stifling. "Why do I always feel like my ears have been boxed whenever I finish a conversation with that woman?"

Carol linked her arm through his and began towing him toward the door. "Don't give her any ideas."

As Harvey was eager to get home and see what he could dig up on all three of the names they'd confirmed, he dropped Carol off at Bread on Arrival and told her he'd rather not come in.

"No problem," she assured him as she unfastened her seat belt. "I'm sure Laura and Molly are anxious to hear how things went."

Before she could push the car door open, her phone buzzed and she reached into her pocket to retrieve it. She recognized the caller immediately as the young teaching assistant, Raimie, even though the young woman was practically whispering.

"The police are at the house next to the school," Raimie blurted. "The empty one the town owns. The kids are in an uproar about it."

"I know the house you mean," Carol said, wondering why the woman would call her about it.

"It has me wondering if someone broke in," Raimie went on. "Maybe even the same someone who was here at the school. Could it have something to do with the break-in and the dead woman?"

"I don't know," Carol said—but she was determined to find out.

15

As soon as Raimie hung up, Carol recounted the call to Harvey. "I'm going to text Molly to let her know, then I'm going over there. If you need to get going, that's fine. I can take my car."

"And miss this?" Harvey asked. "Have you forgotten I'm a newsman?" He pulled back onto the street and headed for Loch Mallaig Elementary.

"I didn't want to assume anything," Carol replied as she quickly typed a message to Molly, apologizing for being late and explaining what was going on.

"Some things you can simply assume," Harvey said.

Sliding her phone into her coat pocket, Carol asked, "Do you suppose this is related to Meg's death?"

"It's a strong possibility. An empty property next to the school would be a tempting place to squat," Harvey said. "As long as you don't let any light shine out through the windows, there's a good chance no one will find you."

Carol gasped softly, drawing a questioning glance from Harvey. "What if another body is there? Grizela hasn't seen Doris since Meg died. What if Meg wasn't the only person who died that night?"

"That is a huge leap," Harvey said, but Carol noticed he picked up speed slightly.

When they reached the school, they immediately saw what Raimie had described. Three police cars were parked in the driveway leading up to the empty house. Harvey pulled off the road and Carol hopped out almost before they came to a full stop. She'd spotted Greer Anderson.

Greer was tucking a wayward strand of blonde hair under her hat as Carol approached. She groaned. "Do you three have a police scanner at the bakehouse or something?"

"Nope," Carol said. "Do you think we need one?"

Greer crossed her arms over her chest. "Apparently not."

"Does this property have anything to do with Meg Shumway's death?" Carol asked bluntly. She saw no reason to ease into the questioning. Greer would either answer or she wouldn't.

Harvey joined them as Greer was replying. "We know someone was squatting here. And we found some of the items stolen from the school. However, we didn't find anything that proved the squatters were Meg and her friend."

"But it would be another disturbing coincidence if they weren't the ones staying here," Harvey said.

"Possibly." Greer frowned at him. "Do you have any idea what would happen to me if the deputy chief caught me chatting with a member of the press?"

"Harvey's retired," Carol insisted.

"Semi," Harvey threw in.

"Then I'll get semifired," Greer replied drily. "I'm not talking to you. Go away."

Carol caught Harvey's eye and tilted her head toward the car. He gave her a look that assured her they would discuss this later, then walked away.

"What stolen items did you find?" Carol asked when Harvey was out of earshot.

"You think talking to the wife of a member of the press will keep me out of trouble?"

"I think you want to talk about this frustrating case."

Greer's mouth twisted, but finally she cracked. "The sleeping mats from the kindergarten class were in there. We also found some old clothes, though we can't be sure whether those were from the school. Honestly, we couldn't get a definitive list. I wonder if we'd even have learned about the break-ins if it had been up to the principal."

"I've gotten the impression she wants to try to do better," Carol said. "And she does have a reason to be afraid of community response."

Greer's interest sharpened. "You're well informed."

"I ran into her at The Hamper last night, right after I talked to you. She was much calmer and more agreeable than she was previously."

"You should have filmed it," Greer grumbled. "I'd have paid money to see that. At any rate, we've been looking into Margaret Shumway, and she *was* originally from Loch Mallaig."

"We were fairly sure that was true."

"Of course you were."

"We're also fairly sure that Meg's friend is Doris Layville Barnside," Carol offered, as Greer pulled her notepad from her coat pocket.

"How sure?"

"With your confirmation of Meg's identity, I'd say somewhere around ninety-five percent." Carol waited as Greer wrote that down. "There is a problem."

Greer glanced up, her expression guarded. "What problem?"

"Doris's family has apparently been telling a story of her death for years," Carol said. "But we showed Grizela a yearbook photo of Doris Layville, and she said the girl in the photo resembled the woman who'd been with Meg at the library, and also reminded her of a teacher at the elementary school."

Greer mulled this over for a moment. "Has she been to the library since Meg's death?"

"Grizela says she hasn't." Carol jerked a thumb toward the house. "You'd tell me if you'd found a second body in there, right?"

"Not if I could avoid it," Greer muttered. "But we didn't. I hate the thought of both these women being from Loch Mallaig. I don't like it, but the deputy chief thinks they probably had a falling-out over something and Doris killed Meg. You hear about that kind of thing all the time in cities, but I never thought I'd see it in Loch Mallaig."

Carol didn't know how to respond. The closer they'd come to tracking down the identity of Doris and Meg, the less Carol had even entertained the idea that Doris could have been the killer. She felt a pang for Kendra. If she did believe her mother was dead, how horrible would it be to learn she was both alive and a killer? Carol profoundly hoped the deputy chief's theory wasn't true.

"Carol, I have to go," Greer said. "If you learn things we should know, call me."

Carol agreed, and the younger woman headed up the drive toward the house.

In the car, Harvey was unsurprised by the deputy chief's theory. "It *is* logical."

"I don't care. I don't want it to be true," Carol said. "If it is, there cannot possibly be a happy ending here. I hate that."

"It's hard to find a happy ending in someone's murder," Harvey replied, and they spent the rest of the drive to Bread on Arrival in silence.

When they reached the bakery, Harvey put a hand on Carol's arm before she got out. "I'm going to keep trying to track down Doris," he said. "And I'm not giving up on that death certificate. Sure, it sounds like she's alive, especially with Grizela's identification of the photo, but I want to know for sure before we stir up so much pain in that family. And it's still possible Kendra's grandparents truly believe their daughter died. If I could find some kind of death notice, it would help."

"I agree." Carol gave him a peck on the cheek and hopped out into the cold for the short walk to the refuge of the warm bakehouse. She entered through the front, happy to see that contented customers filled about half the chairs around the room. That wasn't a bad crowd at all for almost noon in the middle of winter.

"Nice of you to join us again," Hamish grumbled as she walked by.

She merely smiled at him, speaking barely loud enough for him to hear, but not loud enough for the words to carry to the patrons. "I missed you too, Hamish."

That brought on a flurry of bluster, and Carol simply sailed on to the kitchen. She found Molly packaging cookies in a bakery box and Laura carefully rolling a thin chocolate sponge cake around a whipped cream filling.

"You two are so industrious, I'm racked with guilt," Carol said as she shucked off her coat.

"We'll forgive you if you give us a thorough report," Molly said. "We've been dying of curiosity." She held up the box of cookies. "Also, I made the allergen-free cookies for the school you mentioned."

"Thanks," Carol said, smiling at her helpful friend. "I know the teachers will appreciate them."

"I want it noted for the record," Laura announced, "that my curiosity is completely under control."

"Sure," Molly said, then dropped her voice to a stage whisper. "You should have seen her perk up when we heard you coming down the hall."

"I promise to do my best to assuage everyone's curiosity," Carol said. "Whether it was life-threatening or under complete control." She launched into what she'd learned since leaving the bakery with Harvey, trying her best not to leave out anything related to Meg, Millie, or Doris. She finished with, "Greer seemed at the end of her rope, quite frankly. Instead of scolding me for our questions, she actually asked me to let her know if I find anything."

"Poor Greer," Molly said sympathetically. "She loves her job, and she's good at it, but it must be hard sometimes. We mostly deal with people during their happiest moments and provide them with treats. She has to deal with folks at their worst."

"I don't agree with the deputy chief's theory about Doris though." Carol grabbed an apron and tied it on. "I don't want to think of that being the ending."

"It isn't out of the realm of possibility," Laura replied, her tone gentle. "We've all lived in big cities. We know that the most vulnerable people can be pushed into desperate acts."

Molly set her box of cookies on the rack with other items for delivery. "But even in cities, people can get help."

"True," Laura agreed. "But you can't force them to."

Carol wasn't sure. "Sometimes people get too beaten down to believe in help anymore. But even if Doris and Meg were in that spot, they'd been friends since they were kids. I don't want to think of that kind of relationship going bad." She couldn't imagine a situation where she'd hurt Laura or Molly.

"Maybe it was an accident," Molly said. "But let's not talk about that anymore. It makes me feel like crying. I always do when I can't figure out how to help." She straightened her shoulders with apparent resolve. "At least we're trying with the clothing drive. We can help remind folks in bad times that they're still worth having nice things."

"Yes," Laura agreed. "Molly, tell her about Bonnie."

"Bonnie?" Carol echoed.

"Bonnie Findlay came in while you were gone, while Hamish was on a short break and I was up front," Molly said. "I was so excited to see her that I couldn't help myself. I told her all about the coat drive."

"That's not a problem," Carol said, pleased to see Molly's face bright and happy. "It was never meant to be a secret."

"Good," Molly said. "Bonnie was over the moon about it. She says she tries so hard to make donated clothes nice again, but sometimes it's challenging."

"Bonnie Findlay has a good heart and she does put in a lot of hours with The Closet," Laura put in. "She's not afraid to pitch in if it will help someone. She's like her husband that way."

"She is," Carol agreed. "Speaking of pitching in, Fergus said he wants to donate some money to the drive. Molly, he wants you to buy some nice coats and put them in for him."

Molly beamed. "That will be fun. You'll have to come with me, Laura. You have such great taste and with all your experience with The Closet, you'll know the sizes and styles people ask for too."

"Sounds great to me," Laura said.

"Fergus is the best," Molly said, her eyes gleaming with pride.

"Now, there I must step in," Carol said. "Harvey is easily the best guy in the world."

"Harvey's great," Molly said diplomatically. "But . . ."

Carol and Molly turned to Laura, the implication plain—Laura should break the tie. To Carol's amusement, Laura was openly horrified for a second and didn't know what to say. Carol expected her to mention Trent, but that would open her up to some teasing.

Hamish took the pressure off Laura by stomping into the kitchen. He slapped a piece of paper down on the counter. "An order for cupcakes by the end of the day from Mrs. Benchley for her book club tonight. I asked her if she could have waited any longer to place the order and she bit my head off." He harrumphed. "Women."

Laura adopted a smug smile. "You're both wrong. Hamish is the best."

Hamish blinked at her in bewilderment, making all three women laugh. With a scowl, Hamish left the kitchen again, and Carol walked over to pick up the order slip. Cupcakes were right up her alley.

They focused on work for the rest of the afternoon, and Carol was pleased to get the cupcakes baked, cooled, and frosted by the time Mrs. Benchley intended to pick them up. Unfortunately, the woman called to say she couldn't come to the bakehouse and asked for a delivery. Hamish was almost poetic in his rant about that.

Making cupcakes had kept Carol's mind busy for a while, but now she was feeling a little restless. A question had popped into her head, and it insisted on spinning round and round. *If Doris has been staying at the abandoned house, where is she now?*

Molly had continued preparing all the late afternoon orders that needed delivery, then packaged a few more orders for the mail. "Should I ask Hamish if he wants to do deliveries?" she asked. "He parked in the lot after the morning drop-offs, so I think he assumes he's going back out. I could watch the front for the last little bit before we close."

"No," Carol said. "Let me do it. I could use the drive time to clear my head."

"Still thinking about Doris?" Laura asked.

"Mostly wondering," Carol said. "If she and Meg were squatting in the abandoned house next to the school, where is she now? The weather isn't quite as cold as it was, but you still wouldn't be able to sleep out in it."

"Maybe she approached Kendra," Molly suggested. "She could have admitted who she was and sought shelter. She *is* her mother."

Carol hadn't thought of that. "What do you think?" She looked at Laura.

Her friend shrugged. "I suppose it's possible."

Carol wondered if there was a way to find out that didn't involve asking the schoolteacher directly, thus letting the cat out of the bag if the poor woman didn't know her mother was alive. Staking out Kendra's home sounded creepy. *Maybe Harvey will have some ideas.*

"Are you sure you can get the orders to the right places?" Laura asked. She'd finished up the last of the day's baking chores and was beginning kitchen cleanup. "You are awfully distracted."

"I'll be fine," Carol said. "I promise."

"Let me help you load everything," Molly said.

They started with the items that needed to be secured most carefully in the rear of the bakery's delivery vehicle. When the three women had first considered keeping the vintage hearse and transforming it into a delivery vehicle, they'd planned for carrying even the most delicate baked goods. They even had a special setup to hold wedding cakes safely.

After the more fragile items were in, they stowed the other orders, including the special cookies Kendra had requested, making sure nothing could shift and damage itself or anything else. Finally, Molly dusted off her hands. "That should do it. Are you coming back here after deliveries? I mean coming in, not simply switching vehicles."

"If I can do these deliveries quickly enough," Carol said. "I've left you guys to do all the work all day. The least I can do is help with the cleanup."

"Doing the deliveries is plenty," Molly said. "So I'll see you later, or I'll see you tomorrow." As she closed the door on the back of the hearse, they both heard yapping from Angus's barking lot. "Uh-oh, we've been discovered. I should go give him some pats to hold him over for the last bit before closing and his long walk."

"Give him an extra pat from me," Carol said, walking around the hearse to reach the driver's side door. The big vehicle had been a little intimidating at first, but Carol loved driving it these days. In the summer when the town was full of tourists, the hearse drew the oddest stares as she passed. That always made her laugh.

She grabbed the handle of the door, then paused when she spotted what appeared to be a flyer trapped under one of the windshield wipers.

She tugged the folded paper free, spread it out, and immediately realized it wasn't a flyer at all. It was a note, typed in all capital letters. It was only three words, but somehow Carol felt immediately chilled anyway. She read the words over and over, until the sight was permanently etched into her mind.

LEAVE THINGS ALONE.

16

Carol managed to smile and chat each time she dropped off a delivery, but she never completely shook off the effects of the ominous note. When she stopped at the elementary school, she found Kendra had already left for the day, but Raimie was in the classroom, and her delight at the allergen-free treats almost chased away Carol's disquiet. Almost, but not quite. Though Raimie mentioned the commotion at the empty house, Carol merely told her that the police had found the mats from the kindergarten room there.

"Oh." Raimie wrinkled her nose. "I hope the school doesn't decide the kindergarten teachers should still use them."

"I'm sure they won't," Carol said, then begged off further conversation by saying she had cupcakes to deliver. Raimie gushed over the box of cookies again, and Carol made a mental note to tell Molly how much she'd delighted the teacher's assistant.

With each delivery, Carol felt more impatient to return to the bakehouse and show the note to Laura and Molly, but she worked hard not to let her impatience show. She even listened calmly to a lengthy complaint from Mrs. Benchley about Hamish's attitude and the sad state of the service industry in general. Still, through it all, she felt a slight tremor inside every time she thought of the note she'd folded up and stuffed in her pocket. She'd handled it with her gloves on, and she wondered if she should take it to the police. Maybe she would—after she talked to Molly and Laura.

At the bakehouse, Laura was shrugging into her coat and chatting with Molly when Carol walked in. Molly held Angus and rubbed his ears.

"I have something to show you," Carol said as she pulled the note from her pocket, still careful to touch it with her gloved fingers. Unfolding it was a little awkward with the gloves on, but she finally laid it on the shipping table with the bold message easy to read.

"Where did you find that?" Molly asked. She leaned over to examine the note, prompting Angus to lick her chin while it was in range of his tongue.

"Under the windshield wiper on the hearse." Carol hugged herself with a shudder.

"Which suggests the writer intended it for any of us," Molly said. "Or all of us."

"All three of us found Meg," Laura added. "I assume this note is about her death."

"I don't know what else we've been involved in that anyone could object to." Carol eased closer to Molly so she could scratch Angus's ears. There was something comforting about the little dog's fearless expression.

"Unless someone is radically against the coat drive," Molly said and handed Angus to Carol, apparently sensing her friend's distress. "But what specific thing triggered it?"

Carol hugged the little dog. "I don't know. I've been pretty busy today. Maybe someone saw me showing the yearbooks to Grizela or talking to Greer. We would have been easily visible through the school windows."

"Why not leave the note then, when you were away from the car?" Molly asked.

"That's the thing," Carol said. "Greer didn't want to be seen talking to a journalist, so Harvey spent most of the time waiting in the car. That means the person would have *had* to come here to leave the note."

"Then why not put it on your car?" Laura asked.

"Because I wasn't in my car at the school. Harvey drove the SUV. So if someone came here to put it on the car they saw, it wasn't around. The hearse would have been where we'd be sure to see it."

Angus seemed to feel that he'd had enough hugging and began to squirm.

"That's logical," Laura agreed, "but what do we do about it? Did you call the police?"

Carol shook her head as she put the Scottie on the floor, where he sat beside her leg. "I wasn't sure it would be important. There's no threat and no specifics. I feel I know what the person is talking about, but I doubt the police can act on it."

"Still, they should have it," Molly said. "I could give it to Greer at our Piping Yoopers rehearsal tonight if you want to leave it with me."

Carol shivered in the warm room. "I certainly don't want the thing. I feel this pressure to do something, but I don't know what. Harvey is searching for information about the three girls from the high school, but I want something to do."

"My grandfather used to say that there's only one way to make a journey," Laura said. "You have to begin at the beginning."

"And that means?" Molly prompted.

"Honestly, I never figured that out," Laura admitted. "But in this situation, maybe we need to concentrate on the beginning."

"The murder?" Molly asked.

"No," Carol said. "The break-ins at the school. I believe Doris and Meg were breaking in, probably to get things to help them survive the winter. We know that because Greer said some of the items in the house came from the school. But we still don't know *how* they got in. We've been ignoring the break-ins since the murder."

"Could there be a secret way into the school that three former troublemakers from Loch Mallaig would know?" Laura asked.

"I remember knowing a good bit about the school I went to as a kid. Some of it was even true."

"Unfortunately, I'm not from Loch Mallaig," Carol said. "I lack that kind of insider knowledge. I could ask the twins, I suppose. They always have interesting ideas."

"Maybe Fergus would know," Molly said. "He's lived here his whole life, and I'm sure he got into at least a little mischief in his school years."

"If Fergus had known of a secret way into the school, wouldn't he have checked that when we were there Saturday night?" Laura asked.

Molly drooped a little. "I suppose he would have."

"There is one obvious way into the school after hours," Carol suggested. "Someone let them in."

"Who would have done that?" Molly asked. "In fact, who could have? We know the teachers don't have keys to the school."

"And we know that because the one person who lets people in and out of the school told us," Carol said.

The three of them chorused the name together. "Jed Collum."

"I am going to drive back to the school," Carol said decisively as her eyes darted to the clock to be certain she had time. She felt better having a plan. "I want to ask Jed a few questions."

"Don't go alone," Laura said. "I have a meeting with the business association and I promised Trent I'd take notes since he's out of town. Still, I could skip out. I don't want you going by yourself."

"I'm meeting Fergus," Molly said. "But I could call and have him meet us at the school." She looked down ruefully. "We'll have to take Angus too. I can't stick him upstairs without a walk."

Carol appreciated her friends' support more than she could say. "Don't change your plans," she said, waving them off. "Harvey will keep me safe."

Laura finished buttoning her coat. "You promise you won't go without him?"

"Promise," Carol said, tracing an *X* over her heart with a finger.

"In that case, I need to get going on Angus's walk," Molly replied, relief evident on her face. She bent and clipped a leash to his collar. "You two be careful, okay?"

"Definitely." Then Carol remembered what she'd intended to tell Molly. "Oh, and Molly? Raimie was thrilled with the cookies. Thanks so much for taking care of that."

Molly beamed at her. "Always happy to help."

They all left together, Carol and Laura headed for their vehicles while Molly and Angus made their way toward Dumfries Park.

As soon as Carol had closed the car door against the cold and cranked the engine, she called Harvey. "Can you meet me at the school?"

"Don't tell me the police are there again."

"No. I want to have a word with Jed Collum." She explained about the note and her conversation with Laura and Molly. "Laura's right that we're ignoring the original question. How did Meg and Doris get into the school?"

"That's a big one," he agreed. "I'm putting on my coat now. I should be at the school directly. Do not go in without me."

"Yes, sir," Carol said at his fierce tone. "I'll see you there." As she pulled out of the parking lot, she switched on the car's heater and delighted in the blast of warmth. The drive down Tattie Bogle Road curved along the outside of Dumfries Park. Through the bare trees, Carol caught glimpses of Loch Mallaig beyond, though the water was dark and ominous in the late afternoon light. In the summer, that same lake would be full of boats and tourists. It was amazing the difference a few months made.

A few minutes later, Carol pulled into the school parking lot and saw a few scattered cars. She pulled her scarf tighter around her neck and tugged on her knit hat before hopping out. She didn't see the SUV yet, but she knew Harvey would be along directly. She saw no reason to wait in the car since she wouldn't be alone with the custodian in the school building. There were always after-hours tasks that kept at least a few teachers lingering.

Carol walked past the gymnasium side entrance and to the double doors that entered the school near the office. She would wait inside the warm entryway until she saw Harvey pull in.

Unfortunately, so soon after the doors had been held open while children poured out, the entryway didn't offer the warmth she had hoped for, but it did block the chilly late afternoon breeze and gave her a clear view of her car. She knew Harvey would likely park near her, so she should be able to see him.

As she waited, she thought of how the scent of the school building had changed from what she remembered from her own childhood. Back then, the halls always smelled of floor wax and chalk. Now, most of the classrooms had dry-erase boards, and it was rare to find a child who didn't have a computer or electronic tablet—a far cry from the notebooks and writing utensils she'd once carried.

"What are you doing here?"

Carol startled at the sharp voice and spun around. Principal Dour stood outside the office with a leather briefcase in one hand and her coat folded over her arm. The reasonable, even conciliatory attitude the woman had shown at The Hamper was gone. Instead, she was as imperious and unpleasant as Carol remembered.

"I'm waiting on my husband," Carol said honestly, knowing that would not appease the woman.

"If the two of you have a meeting with your grandchildren's teacher, I can assure you that Ms. Layville has gone home for the day. Her classroom is empty."

"I'm not here for Kendra," Carol said, still having no intention of explaining herself outright. She suspected the principal would come up with some reason why she wasn't allowed to see the school custodian. And she rather doubted Jed would tell her anything if he thought the principal knew of the conversation.

The principal strode over, close enough that Carol could see her eyes narrow. "I am the principal of Loch Mallaig Elementary School. Tell me the nature of your presence here at once."

The fierce defiance in the woman's eyes suddenly clicked. It didn't matter that the woman's hair was now silver. It didn't matter that her nose was considerably smaller. Carol had no doubts at all. "You were Millie Fordyce, the third Wild'un!"

17

The principal gasped, her face going ashen. Her eyes darted down the hallway before she grabbed Carol by the arm and began dragging her toward the office, shushing her all the way.

Before Carol and the principal could vanish into the office, Carol heard the heavy front door burst open and Harvey's familiar voice bellow, "Let go of my wife right this second!"

"It's okay, Harvey," Carol said as the principal dropped her arm as if it were hot. "This is Mill—"

The principal shushed her. "Please, come into my office. I'll tell you whatever you want to know, but not in the hall."

The suspicion on Harvey's face didn't lessen, but he followed Carol and Principal Dour into the office without further remark. She could tell by the clenching of his jaw and in his rigid shoulders that he was ready to react immediately if the principal had a weapon in there.

She didn't. Or, at least, not one she showed them. Instead, she closed the door behind them and immediately wilted. "Yes, I'm Millie Fordyce, or I was. But I want to make one thing perfectly clear: those days are far behind me."

"We didn't come here to upset you," Carol said. "In fact, we didn't come to speak to you at all. It wasn't until you were talking to me in the hall that I realized who you were. It must have been a shock when your two school friends showed up in town."

The worry on the principal's face dropped away, replaced by utter shock. "What are you talking about?"

"Meg and Doris," Carol said.

The other woman shook her head firmly. "That's not possible. Doris died years ago. Her daughter told me."

"So you knew that Kendra was your old friend's daughter?" Harvey asked.

"Yes, of course," the principal said.

"Someone in Loch Mallaig has made a possible identification of a woman as her," Harvey said.

Camilla gaped at them. Her mouth worked several times before she managed to stammer, "D-Doris could be alive? And here with Meg?"

Carol felt terrible about what she had to say next, so she spoke as gently as she could. "Meg is the woman we found in the school parking lot on Saturday night."

The color drained from the principal's face, and she swayed on her feet.

Harvey quickly caught the woman by the arm. "You should sit." He guided her to a bench along one wall of the office.

She sank down on it heavily and put her head in her hands. Carol knew no actress was that good. Camilla Dour, formerly Millie Fordyce, had not known the tattered woman in the parking lot was her old friend.

Carol and Harvey stood quietly, giving the woman a moment to recover. Finally the principal spoke, her voice weak. "Do you think Meg was the person you saw inside the school? Maybe she was coming here for help."

Harvey eased behind Carol, silently communicating his belief that the conversation would be smoother if she led it.

"We cannot be entirely sure," Carol said. "But the police did find items from the school inside the empty house next door."

"Oh." Camilla began to shake her head slowly as if somehow rejecting what she was hearing. "I've felt so guilty for not staying in touch, for not knowing that Doris had died until Kendra told me. But now you tell me that Kendra lied to me about it."

"No," Carol said firmly. "I don't believe Kendra is lying. But she may have been lied to by her grandparents. We haven't contacted them yet." She took a breath and continued, "We don't yet know the circumstances of how Doris left Kendra's life. Her grandparents may have felt it was kinder to let the child believe her mother died."

The principal blinked. "How could that be kinder?"

"I don't care to speculate," Carol said.

Again, the principal began shaking her head. "I don't understand any of this. Surely if Doris is in town, she would contact her daughter."

"She's been gone for many years," Carol replied. "And from what we've seen, her circumstances aren't great. Maybe she's ashamed. And now with Meg's death, she could be afraid of bringing that to Kendra's door."

Even as she spoke, Carol wondered what Kendra's reaction would be to finding out her mother wasn't dead. Kendra was a lovely person, but she didn't strike Carol as a pushover. It was entirely possible she would be furious, especially if Doris had simply left her behind. And that led to the big question: What might that anger drive Kendra to do? She hated having Kendra on her mental suspects list, but she didn't see any way around it.

Carol shook her head, realizing silence had fallen in the room. She raised an eyebrow at the principal. "You were resistant to our checking into the break-ins."

"I explained that," Camilla protested.

Carol held up a hand. "Yes, you did. But Meg and Doris were living rough, so it's not unlikely that it was them. We know whoever broke in was living next door in that house. You had no idea anyone was there?"

The principal shook her head. "It's not part of my job to be caretaker to that old house. I suppose I glance in that direction now and then when I'm crossing the lot to my car. If I'd seen lights, I would have taken note, but it's not something I normally think about. I wish I had known. Meg and Doris wouldn't have had to sleep in an unheated house. I would have taken them home with me. I have a perfectly nice house, and I'm all alone in it since my husband died a few years ago. They would have been safe and warm." Her lower lip trembled.

Carol changed the subject in an attempt to keep Camilla from going to pieces. "We came here today to talk to Jed," Carol said. "He has the keys to this building. If he knew that one of the women was an old friend of yours and was Kendra's mother, would he have let them in here?"

"Why would he do that?" the principal asked. "Why not tell me?"

"You're an intimidating woman," Harvey said. "And Jed is a man who avoids conflict. Anyone can see that."

In response to Harvey's words, she stood. "Kendra doesn't have a key to the building, or I would question whether she could be the one letting in the women. But Jed is not out of the question. He's a sweet man, but since he was talked into letting you lot in for your little sleuthing party on Saturday, obviously he is easy to persuade."

"If it helps," Carol said, "he clearly wasn't comfortable with his part in Saturday night's activities."

"You needn't worry," Camilla said. "I have no interest in losing Jed. He is an excellent custodian. He doesn't complain. He works hard. And he maintains a pleasant but appropriately distant relationship with the students."

"I believe we need to speak with Jed," Harvey said.

The principal squared her shoulders and gave Harvey a crisp nod. "Fine. I will take you to him. Please do not intimidate the man."

Carol almost laughed aloud. If Jed was intimidated by anyone, it would be by Camilla herself, not the MacCallans. But she kept this to herself. "We will try to be considerate."

The principal tugged at the front of her wool coat, as if making sure the lines were perfect, then she led them out of the office.

Once they were in the hall, Harvey spoke up. "I believe it best if we go alone."

"Why would you feel that way?"

"You have a formidable presence," Harvey said. "And Jed is going to worry about saying the wrong thing if you're there. I believe he will be more open with us."

"You don't think he'll feel ganged up on?" the woman asked. "With two of you and no one from the school there to support him?"

"We will do our best to ensure he doesn't," Carol said diplomatically.

After several moments of silent deliberation, Camilla said, "Fine. I will bow to your experience in getting information from people, Mr. MacCallan. I will wait in my office. I do ask that you come by and tell me what you learn from him."

"We will come to the office as soon as we are done," Carol assured her.

Camilla checked her watch. "In that case, I believe you'll find him in the lower wing. That is usually where he begins his cleaning for the day."

"Thank you for your understanding and trust," Harvey said and gave the woman an almost courtly bow before taking Carol's hand and heading away from the office.

Once they were around the corner, Carol whispered, "The bow was laying it on a little thick."

"You think?" Harvey asked. "I don't believe I've ever met anyone who was more of a queen ruling her kingdom in my life."

As they walked hand in hand, he slowed his pace. "So, about the fishing trip."

"Really?" Carol asked. "Right now?"

"We have this long hall and probably another before we'll see Jed," Harvey said. "That's plenty of time. Have you made a decision about the trip? Have you talked to Molly and Laura?"

Carol huffed, more in exasperation than from the walk. "I don't know what I want to do. I don't want to leave town while there is an open murder investigation connected to the twins' school."

He gave her a side-eyed glance. "You think I'd even think about leaving if I thought any of this put the twins in danger?"

"Can you be sure it doesn't?"

He pulled her to a stop. "We can never be sure any moment is completely free of danger. We live in a complicated world, but I feel fairly confident. Are you hesitating for fear of the twins or because you don't want to leave questions unanswered?"

"Of course I don't enjoy leaving unanswered questions," Carol said, tugging her hand out of his grasp. "You know me better than that. But I also feel as if I'd be leaving the twins here with a dark shadow way too close to them. I want to see this settled before I go anywhere."

"Well, I hope you don't think I'm going to leave you here alone when you're on a mission," Harvey said. "We both know you don't always look before you leap."

Carol pivoted and continued down the hall. "I can take care of myself."

"Sure," Harvey muttered as he trotted to catch up.

They reached the end of the hall, where another hallway joined in a T-shape. This hall led to the shorter halls of each wing. They turned toward the lower wing, where they'd stood waiting for a possible intruder less than a week before. That's when they realized they had found the person they were seeking—and more.

Jed and Kendra faced off in the middle of the hallway, and Kendra was enraged. She obviously didn't notice that she and Jed weren't alone, as she was completely engrossed in glaring at the distressed custodian.

The first thought that came to Carol was that the principal had insisted Kendra was gone for the day. Apparently the number of things Camilla Dour didn't know were multiplying.

"I can't believe what you did," Kendra said, her voice tight with rage. "And I'm never going to forgive you."

18

As Carol stood beside Harvey and peered down the long hall, it was as if everything froze for a moment and all she could see was Kendra and Jed. Kendra's fists were clenched tightly and tension radiated from her stance. Jed was bowed as if he bore an enormous weight, his back nearly round from his cowed posture.

A tightness in her own chest made Carol realize she'd forgotten to breathe in her astonishment. She drew in a breath as gently as possible, afraid that any movement would draw Kendra's eye and end their chance to learn what was going on.

Almost shaking, Kendra spoke again, punctuating each sentence with a jab of her finger in Jed's chest. "You knew. All this time you knew. How could you think it was anything but wrong to keep this from me?"

Jed took a step away from Kendra. "She asked me not to, begged me."

"And that was more important than my feelings?"

"No," he insisted. "But she wanted to tell you herself."

"Really?" Kendra's voice grew almost shrill. "And did she? Tell me where she is, Jed Collum! I have a right to know, a right I've had all this time."

Carol caught the movement behind Kendra's back even before the disheveled woman stepped out of the art room. Her resemblance to Kendra was striking, as if the woman in the bulky, tattered clothing was the image of what Kendra could be after years of bad times.

"Yes, child," Doris said. "You've had that right."

Kendra spun with a shriek and jumped away from her mother, nearly colliding with Jed. If she noticed the near collision, Kendra showed no sign of it. Her eyes were fixed on Doris.

Carol didn't realize she'd taken a step forward until Harvey's hand rested on her shoulder. She had so many questions for this woman. But she stopped. Harvey was right. Kendra's answers needed to come first.

"Who are you?" Kendra asked, sounding as hollow as the wind off Loch Mallaig, and nearly as cold.

"I'm your mother," Doris answered.

"No!" Kendra shouted, her hands curling into fists. "My mother *died*!"

"I didn't." Doris spoke now as if each word was broken glass, cutting her even as she said them. "I lived. Your father died."

"What are you talking about?" Kendra said through gritted teeth.

"I was driving, you see." Doris's low voice was saturated with heartache. "He usually drove, but I had to insist that we share the driving. I called him a control freak over it. Your father and I, we didn't argue much, but there must have been something in the air that night. I got my way. I drove. And I lost my love. They said the accident wasn't my fault, but if he'd been in the driver's seat, he'd be alive. I do know that."

"You lost Dad, but you had me," Kendra said, the pain of the woman's story clearly not diminishing her anger.

"I did. You were a shining light, sure enough, but I'd gone blind with sadness," Doris said. "I was broken. Losing your father, knowing he died because of my stubbornness, it broke me. It broke me so bad I didn't have anything left for my baby girl, and she deserved the world."

"So you abandoned me?"

"I left you where you would be safe and warm and loved, as you deserved," Doris said. "I ran away, knowing your grandparents would make sure you had all the love in the world, because that's what they'd given me. And I knew I couldn't give it, not with my heart broken and empty."

Carol saw tears tracking down Kendra's face, but then the scene blurred and Carol had to dash away her own tears.

"So why are you here now?" Kendra asked.

Doris exhaled, a long, shuddering rattle. "Because Meg and I thought it was time to tell the truth."

"The truth that you'd abandoned me?" Kendra asked.

"That, and a whole lot more."

"How much more?" Carol asked finally, walking down the hall before Harvey could restrain her. "What truth did you and Meg bring? Was it big enough for someone to kill Meg? Do you know who did it?" *Was it you?* The last question pushed against Carol's lips, but she swallowed it. For now.

Doris put her hands on her hips and looked Carol up and down. Suddenly Carol could see a bit of the wild girl from so many years before. She'd been battered, but she wasn't totally beaten.

"And who are you to be asking me so many questions?" Doris demanded.

Jed slunk toward Carol, his eyes darting from side to side. "Can we please have this conversation somewhere besides the hallway? I don't know if my boss has left yet."

"She hasn't," Carol said. "She's in her office."

The man's expression grew almost frantic. "Please, can we go somewhere else?" He cast about frantically. "We could go to the basement. No, that won't work. The door down there is too close to the office. Does the principal know you're here?"

"She does," Carol said as Harvey came to her side.

"Jed, breathe," Doris said, and none of the earlier brokenness showed on her now. She waved a hand toward the art room. "We can talk in my office."

Harvey actually laughed at that, drawing a scowl from nearly everyone in the hall.

As before, the art room was a profusion of brightly colored chaos that smelled strongly of tempera paint and crayons. Tables and easels made the room a maze, and Carol wondered how the children who had class in this room managed not to knock things over regularly.

Ignoring the undersize chairs, Doris leaned against the edge of the art teacher's desk. "I'll tell you everything."

Jed quickly closed the door to the art room, but peered out the small window set high in the door.

"Do you know who killed Meg?" Carol asked.

For a moment, Doris's defiant glare softened to reveal anguish once more. "I don't. I wasn't there. Meg had left the house next door after we had an argument. I wanted to see Kendra, but Meg said we had other secrets to tell first and she'd already started on that. I didn't agree, but Meg was dying. How do you argue with a dying woman?"

"Where was Meg going the night she died?" Harvey asked.

Doris glowered. "And who are you two?"

"They're helping me," Kendra said defiantly. "After all the break-ins by you and your friend, the teachers were scared. We are responsible for young children here, and we didn't know who was trespassing at night."

"Are you police?" Doris asked suspiciously.

"Actually, she's a baker," Harvey said. "And I'm a fisherman."

Carol noticed how he didn't mention being a journalist, but she supposed that knowledge could have made Doris clam up. No one wanted that.

The woman seemed a little confused by Harvey's answer, but then Kendra said, "Just tell us."

Doris relented at once. "If you trust them, then I will too. I don't know where Meg was going. Sometimes she walked because she felt so restless from the pain. She had cancer. Did you know that?"

"We did," Carol admitted. From the corner of her eye, she saw that Kendra was listening to her mother with rapt attention. She might have been angry about the deception, but she was hungry to hear the truth now.

"The pain made it hard for her to settle sometimes, and our arguing made it worse." Doris studied the floor and murmured, "I suppose I make things worse as a habit." She shook herself and raised her head again. "At any rate, Meg didn't come back, so I went searching for her. I thought she would be in here, warming up. She wasn't, but a couple I'd never seen before spotted me, so I left. I went to the house and waited." Her chin trembled. "Turns out I was waiting for a dead woman."

"Doris," Carol said. "Where have you been since Meg died? You weren't at the house next door when the police searched it."

"Jed has been letting me stay in the basement here. It's warm, and I've stayed in worse."

With one question answered, Carol moved on to the next. "The secrets you said Meg wanted to reveal first—would someone kill to keep them buried?"

"I can't imagine why," Doris said, her brow furrowed. "That wouldn't make a lick of sense. If anything, it's keeping the secret that's been bad."

"You need to tell us what that secret is," Carol said.

Doris exhaled. "I suppose I'm going to have to tell this story a lot. May as well get used to it. Since it sounds like you've been poking around, I expect you've heard that Meg, Millie, and I were a little impish in our youth, right?"

"Yes, we've heard," Carol said.

"We weren't mean girls," Doris said. "But we were bad for each other. We brought out the worst in each other. Sometimes people are like that. They're fine on their own, but they're the devil's own gang when they get together."

"And that's how the Wild'uns were?" Harvey asked.

"It is," Doris said. "We'd gotten into pranks that year. Soap in swimming pools, food coloring in the water fountains, and then the big prank."

Carol made the leap even before Doris revealed it. "The cow?"

"The cow," Doris confirmed.

"What cow?" Kendra asked.

"We were mad at the school principal," Doris said. "We must have been down to his office once a week, getting scolded. We probably should have been sent home, but the principal was actually a nice man. He wanted to give us every chance, but we didn't see it that way. We thought he was spoiling our fun."

"So you put a cow in his office," Carol concluded.

"We did," Doris replied. "We nearly gave up on the prank half a dozen times. It's not easy to get a cow halfway across town without a truck. We were lucky we picked a cow that could be led on a rope, but even that depended on giving her treats. But we didn't give up. We were stubborn, and we got the cow into the principal's office."

"And everything went wrong from there," Carol said.

Doris hugged herself, rubbing her arms. "We should have come clean. We knew that. And at different times, each of us wanted to confess, but we never could get that good inclination to sync up. We were scared to death of what would happen to us. And then the football team was blamed. It was perfect, a gift. We were safe. Guilty, but safe."

"What exactly went wrong?" Kendra asked. "I don't know this story."

"A custodian let the cow out," Harvey said. "And it trampled him. He was badly hurt."

Kendra's hand flew to her mouth. "Oh no." Her gaze settled on her mother.

"Yes, baby, I did that. I guess I've had a wrong streak my whole life." Doris focused on Harvey. "No one suspected us, I suppose because we were a bunch of girls. We were never even questioned. If we had been, every single one of us would have cracked. We were fragile as hollowed-out eggs after it happened. One nudge and we would have cracked, but no one nudged us. Our parents thought the town was full of hooligans, and they worried we'd be led astray. They had no idea."

"So you all moved." Harvey raised an eyebrow. "That is an extreme response. Are you sure they didn't suspect?"

"I can't say for Meg's folks or Millie's either, but I don't think mine did," Doris answered. "At least they never acted as if they did. They didn't see any harm in us, and we sure didn't want to hurt anyone."

"Good intentions don't always produce good results," Kendra said. "Gram says that a lot."

Doris's eyes shone with welling tears. "Sounds like Mom." Frowning, she continued. "Once we'd moved, there wasn't anyone to tell. But sometimes knowing I'd done this terrible thing—it would fester inside and wake me up with these awful stomachaches. I could push it down, but it kept coming back. Even after I married. Even after I had my baby girl. I had this sick feeling that this bad thing I'd done was simply waiting to pop up and ruin my life. Then, a few years after your dad died, when I ran into Meg in the city, I found out it did the same to her. Even after all these years."

"I'm glad!" Everyone turned to stare at Jed in shock. He'd moved away from the door to face Doris more directly and his posture was anything but timid now. "I'm glad you felt something, because what you did was bad."

"I know," Doris said. "We didn't mean any harm."

"But you did harm," Jed insisted. "My dad never fully recovered."

"Your dad?" Carol and Harvey spoke in unison. Carol's head was spinning from the revelation, and she exchanged a glance with Harvey. *Did you see this coming?*

His expression mirrored the shock she felt.

"My dad was the custodian then," Jed said. "He had to go to the hospital, and he couldn't do this work anymore. Dad loved his job. He was good at it, and he shouldn't have ever been hurt. He wouldn't have hurt you."

"No," Doris said. "He wouldn't. I should have seen him in you, Jed. You don't favor him much, but you have the same kind eyes. I didn't even know your dad's real name. He used to tell folks his name was Swabbie because he did so much mopping in the Navy. They even used to call him that way over the intercom. 'Mr. Swabbie to the gym.' Why didn't you tell me that you were Mr. Swabbie's son?"

"Because I didn't know you were one of the people who put a cow in the office," Jed said. "I thought you were just Kendra's mother."

"So you were the one who let Doris and Meg into the school?" Carol asked.

He scuffed the toe of one boot against the floor. "I did it because she was Kendra's mom. I like Kendra, and I didn't think her mom ought to be out in the cold so much. I told them to get stuff out of the lost and found. No one ever claims that stuff and it gets hauled off eventually. I also told them to take the sleeping mats, because I heard the teachers saying they ought to throw the mats in the trash so the school could authorize new ones. I wanted to help Kendra's mom because Kendra is so nice. She's nice to the kids, and she's always nice to me. She doesn't treat me like I'm stupid, or like she's better than me. A lot of people do that because I clean up after everyone. It's not stupid to enjoy cleaning and making things nice again."

"According to the principal, you do it well," Carol said gently.

Jed's lips quirked up, but only for an instant. His face hardened, and he glared at Doris. "I wouldn't have helped you if I'd known who you are. I'd have left you out in the cold. You don't deserve a nice daughter like Kendra."

"I agree with you there," Doris said quietly.

Carol wondered if this really was the first time Jed had learned about Doris and Meg's link to his father. What if Meg had told him on Saturday night? He was clearly furious about it. Could that anger have gotten out of control? "Jed, did you kill Meg?"

Jed gaped at her, but before he could gather himself for a reply, they all heard a voice from the doorway. "Don't be ridiculous."

They spun to see Camilla Dour standing there, ramrod straight and imperious as ever. She raised her chin. "Jed Collum wouldn't hurt another human being. Period. And if you people had the sense God gave a housefly, you'd know that."

"People can surprise you," Harvey replied stubbornly.

The principal dismissed his remark with a sniff. Instead, she pointed at Jed. "Your dad's story doesn't end with the night at the high school. Tell the rest of it."

19

Carol expected Jed's display of temper to scale down immediately. Standing up to Camilla was no easy task, and Jed had shown no sign of it any other time. But now he jutted out his chin and spoke defiantly. "He was in the hospital for a long time. He thought he might die."

The principal didn't react, merely watching him without expression. "And?"

Jed shoved his hands in the pockets of his coveralls, his tone mildly grudging as he continued. "He said it made him realize what a good town this was because so many people pitched in to help him. He said he got so many flowers the nurses called his room 'the jungle.' Dad thought that was funny."

"And?" Camilla repeated.

"Someone even fed his cat." This last was nearly mumbled.

The principal waved that off. "I mean, what happened to your father afterward? As it happens, this is a story I've followed rather closely. What happened after your father got out of the hospital?"

For an instant, Jed's temper flared in his eyes again. "He couldn't go to work at the school again. And he missed it. He told me he always missed being at the school, doing his part to keep things right."

The principal didn't even speak this time, just continued to stare at Jed.

"Fine. He got a settlement from the state," Jed said. "But not nearly as much as he got in donations from the town. Since he couldn't go back to being a custodian, he took night classes. He became an accountant, and it paid a lot more. He finally made enough to start a family."

"And you were the result of that," Camilla said. "Weren't you?"

"Well, yeah," Jed said, a little sullenly. "But Dad still limps, especially when it rains or it's cold. And it's cold a lot here."

"Has he stayed angry at the football players?" the principal asked. "The ones people believed guilty at the time?"

"No," Jed said in a voice almost too low to hear. "He says they put his life on the path that brought him here, and he wouldn't give up his family for anything."

"That's what I thought." The principal turned her whole body toward Doris. "You and Meg should have told me you were here instead of squatting in an empty house and breaking into my school. You could have stayed with me."

Doris walked closer to the other woman and peered into her face. "Meg didn't even believe you were you. She said nobody changed that much. She figured it was the world's wildest coincidence."

"And what did you think?" Camilla asked.

Doris shrugged. "Your parents always were the richest. They pay for that nose?"

"That's not your business," Camilla said.

Doris hooted. "You sure have gone uptown, Millie. Why would I possibly think you'd undo that knot in your tail long enough to do anything good for me or Meg?"

"Because we were best friends," Camilla insisted, and something in her tone hinted at the hurt she felt but refused to show. Carol thought it must be hard to put on such a tough facade all day, every day.

Doris didn't comment on the principal's remark. Instead, she said, "You took good care of my girl. Jed says she's a great teacher."

"She is that," Camilla agreed.

"She is also right here," Kendra snapped.

"I know, child," Doris said, then her gaze cut to Carol and Harvey. "You sure stirred up a hornet's nest."

Carol met the woman's eyes without flinching. "I believe it's better for the truth to be out in the open. You can't heal if you hide a wound instead of treating it."

"You've learned all our secrets now," Camilla said. "Have you figured out who killed Meg?"

"No," Carol said. "But I haven't had much time to process the rush of revelations here."

"We do have a large suspect pool," Harvey chipped in. "And plenty of motives to go around."

The others glared at him. What he'd said was true, but Carol wasn't sure it had needed saying. She stepped closer to Doris. "You will need to speak to the police, Doris. They've been searching for you."

Doris became upset. "The police are no friends of mine."

"The police here will treat you fairly," Carol insisted. "No one in Loch Mallaig gets railroaded. They need to know everything about Meg so they can find out who hurt her."

"Can't they figure that out on their own?" Doris asked.

"You want to ignore your duty and hope for the best again?" Kendra asked. "That sounds like a choice you're getting too comfortable with."

"You don't know everything," Doris said. "Can't we talk?"

"Yes, we can and we will," Kendra said, her tone suggesting Doris wouldn't enjoy it much. "But not until after you do what's right with the police. If you want me to let you into my life, you have to stand up for something, for someone. I have to see you do that, to believe you won't cut and run again if things get hard for us someday."

Doris hung her head silently for a long moment with every eye on her. Finally, she met her daughter's gaze. "I'll do it. For you and for

Meg." Then she snorted. "The worst they can do is lock me up, and at least they'll have heat in the building."

"You do that. When they let you go, call me. I'll come get you." Kendra walked over to the art teacher's desk and scribbled her number on a piece of sketchbook paper. She tore it away and handed it to her mother.

"Doris?" Carol said as the other woman stared in wonder at the paper. "I can give you a lift to the station. Surely you've had enough of walking around in Loch Mallaig this winter."

"Thank you." Doris held up the paper. "I'll call you, baby girl. Soon as I'm done, I'll call you."

"I'll be waiting," Kendra replied, and her expression was soft enough that it was almost a smile.

The next morning, Carol left for work early. She'd slept poorly again and was almost glad when it was time to stop tossing and turning and face the day. She had no idea whether Doris was still in police custody, and she had told herself over and over that she could trust the police to be fair to her.

The truth was that Carol still couldn't be sure Doris wasn't the killer. Carol believed the woman's story, but that didn't make her innocent. The whole of Tuesday evening had left her feeling unsettled with an uncomfortable sense of urgency. She *did* believe it was good for the truth to come out, but she also worried about what would happen as a result.

She found Laura in the bakehouse kitchen mixing dough for the morning scones. "Is Molly down yet?" Carol asked.

"She's walking Angus." Laura plopped the dough onto her floured work space, then stopped to study Carol. "Your text message saying you were fine was a little vague yesterday. I thought we would get a follow-up call."

"Sorry, but I was exhausted," Carol said. "I guess I wanted a little time to order my thoughts. It was an eventful school visit to say the least. As soon as Molly gets here, I promise to tell you everything."

Laura raised an eyebrow. "I'll hold you to that. Since we're waiting, can you mix up some blueberry scones while I do the herb-and-cheddar? The blueberry ones have been selling out early, so we should make a double batch. I've thawed and drained extra berries already."

"I'm on it." Carol hung her coat on the rack and tied on an apron. At least mixing the dough should help clear her head.

Carol had mixed her scones and was cutting them to put on the baking sheet when she heard footsteps overhead.

"Molly's back, thank goodness," Laura said. "I have been itching with curiosity since you got here."

Carol smiled. Laura was nearly as good at maintaining her calm as Camilla was. Carol began transferring the scones to the baking sheet, but she kept watching the doorway. She was eager to talk things through with her friends.

Molly practically skipped through the door, waving the *Crown Press News*. "I can't believe you didn't call and tell me all this stuff last night, Carol!"

"The newspaper knows?" Carol asked, snatching the paper and staring at it in horror.

"If gossip counts as knowing," Molly said, rolling her eyes. "They say the police picked up a suspect. From your text, I assume they're talking about Doris."

"She came to them," Carol said. "But Kendra talked her into it."

Laura whistled. "There must have been fireworks."

"More than you can imagine. Especially when we also discovered that Principal Camilla Dour is Millie Fordyce after all." Carol grimaced. "I know I didn't mention that. It was a little complicated for a text." She scanned the newspaper in her hands. "I don't suppose the paper says whether they held Doris?"

"It says they didn't," Molly said. "But they hinted that the police probably should have. They also said, 'an unsolved murder may be linked to one of the town's biggest scandals.' Do you know what they mean by that, Carol?"

"I do," Carol said grimly, handing the paper back to Molly. She recounted the whole experience at the school, from her realization that Camilla Dour was Millie all the way through talking Doris into going to the police. "I don't think Doris killed anyone," she said when she was done. "Seeing her in the school supports her story of searching for Meg during a time the police say Meg was already dead."

"*If* she was hunting for Meg," Laura said. "And not in the school for another reason."

"Always possible," Carol admitted. "But I believe her."

"Which counts for a lot," Molly said. "But what about the principal? Do you think she could have killed Meg?"

"She had motive," Laura chimed in. "Being part of the cow prank wouldn't help her reputation in Loch Mallaig. It could even mean the end of her job."

"That's true," Carol said. "But she was honestly shocked to learn that the dead woman was her old friend from school."

"She could have been lying," Laura pointed out.

"I know." Carol sighed. "They could *all* be lying." She picked up the tray of scones and shoved it into the oven with undue force, frustration making her edgy. She walked to her work space and began wiping up the flour with rough strokes. "None of this makes sense. Jed was furious when he learned Doris was part of the prank that crippled his dad, but he also acted as if it was new information to him. Still, if he's lying, he could be a suspect. We have far too many suspects whose guilt or innocence rests on whether or not they're good liars."

"I'd be a terrible suspect," Molly said. "I can't tell a believable lie to save my life. Almost literally sometimes."

"What about Kendra?" Laura asked. "You said she was angry at her mother. What if she knew about the women's real identities?"

"That would make sense if it was Doris who had been attacked, but Kendra could hardly confuse a white woman with her mother," Carol said.

"I don't know," Molly said. "She was heavily bundled, and her face was probably covered. She wore mittens and a hat over her hair. Seeing that, she could have snuck up on her and killed her before she realized her mistake."

Carol groaned. That sounded entirely too possible. "Thanks, Molly. What we needed here was another suspect."

"Then I have bad news," Laura said.

"What's that?" Carol asked suspiciously.

"We haven't considered another group with a good reason to be angry with Meg," Laura said.

"Who?" Carol and Molly asked in unison.

"The football team," Laura said. "They were blamed for the prank. The custodian was badly injured, but the false accusation injured the team too. Didn't Fergus say that Ballard Maddox, the paramedic, had been in line to receive a big scholarship, but didn't end up getting it?"

Carol drew in a sharp breath. "That's right, and Ballard ended up in a perfect place to conceal evidence as well."

"But would he have even known?" Molly asked. "Fergus didn't recognize the woman as Meg, and he was as close to her as Ballard got."

Carol felt an almost visceral reaction to the new idea. It felt so *true*. "Meg's whole reason for coming to Loch Mallaig was to come clean about the past. And though Doris was reluctant, it's entirely possible that Meg was moving ahead with her plan by coming clean to the people she'd injured the most—the falsely accused."

"So you think she tracked him down and spilled the secret?" Molly asked. "Then why was she killed at the school?"

"Maybe it took some hours of stewing for the rage to boil over," Laura said. "And if she told him where she was staying, it wouldn't have been hard to spot her out walking. Ballard would have known what the new Meg looked like."

Carol shuddered. Had they been within feet of the murderer that night?

20

Laura summed up what they all felt. "We need to visit Ballard Maddox." She waved a hand around the kitchen. "After we finish with morning prep here, of course."

"All of us?" Molly said.

"All of us," Laura said. "I know I don't want to be left behind. I've spent too much time hearing about what's going on around here and not enough time doing something about it."

Carol wasn't sure it was a job for all of them. "Do you think he's going to let three women he doesn't know into his house *and* answer questions?"

Molly smoothed her hands over her apron. "He might," she suggested. "If Fergus was along. After all, they went to high school together."

"Good thought," Laura agreed.

Carol could see the value in having Fergus along, but it meant there would be four people confronting the man. "Can we all even leave? I assume you want to wait until Hamish gets here, but is it fair of us to leave him to work alone without warning?" She tapped the copy of the *Crown Press News* that Molly had brought in. "That kind of reporting always brings in extra people who want a gathering place for gossip."

"That's true," Laura said. "Hamish could get grumpy."

"Grumpier," Molly threw in.

"Grumpier," Laura agreed. "I'll call Bridget and see if she's free to work."

Jan Fields

"Good idea," Molly said. "Bridget has a calming effect on Hamish most of the time. My theory is that he's afraid she'll laugh at his curmudgeon act."

"And she does," Carol said. "But Bridget laughs at most things. It's one of the qualities I enjoy most about her. She appreciates the ridiculousness of life." Then she groaned. "I'll have to call Harvey and tell him what we're planning to do. I don't want to face him afterward if he doesn't know. At least having Fergus along will convince him we'll be safe."

So the three made their calls. Both Laura and Molly's calls resulted in good news. Bridget would come in, though she sensed a mystery afoot and made Laura agree to tell her everything later. Fergus would smooth their way with his old friend. Only Harvey seemed intent on interfering.

"I'm coming with you," he said the second Carol finished telling him the plan.

"Not necessary," Carol said. "There are three of us, and Fergus will be there as well. Plus, we have no evidence that this man has done anything wrong. This may be simply information gathering."

"Good," Harvey said. "I'm great at that. I'll come over to the bakehouse right now so you can't sneak off without me."

"I don't appreciate being treated like a wayward teen."

"I know," Harvey said and ended the call, leaving Carol doubly annoyed at being cut off before she could really swing into her rebuttal.

Molly must have caught sight of Carol's expression because she asked, "What is it?"

"There are moments when I question my life choices," Carol answered in a waspish tone, though she knew she didn't mean it. She loved Harvey and loved being married to him, but it wasn't without challenges. "Harvey's on his way over to go with us."

And he proved true to his word, so Carol put him to work on some of the morning prep. She expected him to complain, but he readily agreed and even whistled while he worked. Carol wondered if that particular choice was supposed to be as annoying as it was. Still, Harvey was helpful, and by the time Hamish showed up, the decks were clear for them to go. As if on cue, Fergus strolled into the kitchen.

"Bridget sent me back," he said. "She's curious as a cat."

"She is," Laura agreed. "I hope what we find out will be worth the suspense we're creating for her."

"For all of us," Molly said.

"Don't expect too much," Fergus said. "I'm certain Ballard Maddox had nothing at all to do with that woman's death. He's dedicated his adult life to helping people."

"Either way," Carol said, "I hope he can tell us something to point us in the right direction."

Fergus was still frowning. "Then we might as well leave." He invited Laura to ride with Molly and him in his Range Rover.

Laura grinned in reply. "I'll take a spot of luxury and have the whole back seat to myself. Unless Carol and Harvey are riding with us?"

"You'd be welcome," Fergus said.

"Thanks," Harvey said, "but we'll drive ourselves."

Swallowing a remark about Harvey choosing for them that she knew was motivated entirely by her annoyance with him, Carol shrugged into her coat and mentally prepared herself to face the freezing cold, even if it was only for a short walk to the car.

The wind was whipping, and every one of them gasped when they stepped outside.

"I'll lead," Fergus said to Harvey. "Can you follow or do you need the address?"

"I can follow," Harvey said. "Are you sure the poor man won't think we're storming the castle?"

"I called him," Fergus said. "He's expecting us."

Molly gave Fergus a sharp glance, suggesting this was news to her, but they trooped to their vehicles without comment.

Harvey waited until they'd pulled out in traffic behind Fergus before he peered sideways at Carol. "What's the bee in your bonnet? Are you still mad that I wanted to come along?"

"I don't have a bee in my bonnet," Carol retorted. "But you're being a little heavy-handed today, don't you think? I'm starting to think a little space while you go on your fishing trip would be a nice breather for us."

The expression he flashed her way was slightly hurt. "I worry about you. That isn't new."

"As long as it doesn't make you forget that we're a partnership," she said.

"Have I ever forgotten that?" He chuckled before she could answer. "Okay, have I ever forgotten that for long?"

"Not for long."

"Then let's table this until after we're done talking to a possible murderer. Okay?"

"Okay." Carol didn't mention that Harvey's thoughts were much like hers. She wasn't sure it was fair to be thinking of Ballard Maddox that way. Fergus didn't. But she wanted so badly for them to find the killer.

The drive to Ballard's house didn't take long. He lived in a quiet neighborhood that Carol couldn't help noticing was within walking distance of the schools and the house Meg had been living in.

When they climbed out of the two vehicles, Fergus took the lead.

Ballard answered the door almost as soon as Fergus's knuckles hit it. "I know why you're here. You may as well come in."

The group exchanged amazed looks. Was it going to be this easy? As soon as Ballard closed the door behind them, he said, "I read the newspaper this morning and saw they dug up the cow thing. I figured you want to talk about that. Someone from the *Crown Press News* called to get my 'statement.' I told him to buzz off. I'll talk to you, though, Fergus." His gaze swept over the group, but he didn't say anything else.

"Maybe we could sit down somewhere?" Fergus asked.

Ballard surveyed the room. "The kitchen table should work. I don't normally entertain so many people at once. You guys want coffee?"

"We're good," Fergus said. "But you can get one for yourself if you want."

"No, I'd rather answer whatever you want to know so I can move on."

They filed along behind him to a large, airy kitchen with a small table. A few folding chairs were leaned against a wall, so Ballard began opening them. "I bought a bunch of chairs because I sometimes have the guys over to play poker or watch football since I have a big TV."

"The guys?" Carol asked.

"The guys from the football team," Ballard explained. "Well, the ones who are left."

"Some moved away?" Laura asked as she sank into one of the chairs.

"Yeah, and one of the guys died," Ballard said.

Carol could almost feel her ears prick up. "How awful."

Ballard spun the last of the folding chairs around and straddled it. "Yeah, it was pretty hard on all of us. Roger played center on the team. You remember, Fergus?"

"Vaguely. He was in the military, right?"

"Yeah. Roger had been counting on a scholarship to get to college, same as me, but they dried up after the cow incident. Roger decided to join the military. He said he could serve a few years, then go to college with the government's help."

"But he didn't do that?" Carol asked.

Ballard shook his head. "He never made it home. He had a new wife too. They'd rushed into marriage on account of Roger leaving, but I believe they would have made it even so. Roger was a good guy, quiet and smart."

"Wow, that must have been horrible for his wife," Carol said. She wondered where the wife was and whether she harbored a grudge against the people whose actions had sent her husband into the military.

"Absolutely," Ballard agreed. "And Roger never even met his kid."

"He had a child?" Laura asked.

Ballard bobbed his head. "He lives here in Loch Mallaig. He even comes to the game nights sometimes, but he doesn't exactly fit in. He's a unique one. Smart like his dad, but growing up without a father was rough on him. The guys tried to be there, but it wasn't the same."

"I barely remember Roger," Fergus said, "and I can't recall his last name."

"Not surprising," Ballard said. "Roger was quiet. He was easy to miss. Anyway, his name was Quayle, Roger Quayle. We sometimes called him The Bird on account of his name."

Carol felt all the air whoosh out of her. Roger Quayle's son was smart, but not the sort who would fit in with Ballard and the guys who hung out from the team. Carol could picture someone who fit that description perfectly. She knew from a quick glance around that she wasn't the first to make the connection, but she was the first to speak. "Is Roger's son named Byron?"

"Yeah, that's him," Ballard said. "His mom had a thing for poetry, especially Lord Byron's."

Carol responded with a slight tilt of her head, her mind spinning. Roger Quayle's son, who'd never met him and had a hard time. He would have known the part the cow prank played in his father's death. "Excuse me," Carol finally managed to say. "I need to make a call."

"Sure," Ballard said. "You need my landline?"

"No, thank you. I have my phone." Carol stood and found her knees were wobbly. She'd thought Ballard would be a good suspect because he lived near the school, but Byron was even closer. He was at the school every single weekday. How easy would it have been for Meg to tell him her secret? How easy would it have been for him to get her alone? And now, with the help of the *Crown Press News*, how easy would it be for him to find a second member of the group he blamed for his father's death?

Harvey stood up beside her. "A call?"

"Jenny," she said, then stepped out of the kitchen and into Ballard's small living room.

Harvey followed. "Why Jenny?"

"I don't know where Kendra lives," Carol said. "But I assume that's where Doris is. And I assume Byron would know the address, or could get it easily enough. I don't want to bother Kendra during school hours, but I know this is Jenny's free period. She'll know where Kendra lives too, since they are friends."

"Good reasoning," Harvey said.

Carol's hands shook slightly as she picked her daughter's name from her contact list. She hoped she wasn't too late. "Jenny?" Carol said as soon as her daughter picked up.

"Hi Mom," Jenny said in a voice that was far too cheery for her daughter. Almost manically cheery. "I can't talk now. I'm visiting the twins' classroom." And then her daughter, whom Carol had raised to be painstakingly polite in all ways, hung up on her.

Carol covered her mouth with one hand and gaped at Harvey. "Something is wrong. I think Jenny is in danger."

21

Carol was still staring at Harvey, trying to sort out what they should do next, when the others came into the room. "What's going on?" Molly asked. "Did you call the police?"

"I called Jenny," Carol said. "I wanted to get Kendra's address, but Jenny sounded strange on the phone. And she says she's visiting the twins' classroom."

"Surely Byron wouldn't try anything at the school," Laura said.

"What are you talking about?" Ballard asked. "What would Byron try?" No one answered him.

"We have to go to the school," Fergus said. "Byron may have lost it. We'll call the police on the way."

"Are you sure?" Carol asked weakly. "We don't *know* that anything is going on."

"I trust your instincts," Fergus said. "You know your daughter."

"We do," Harvey said firmly. "And Carol is right."

"I'm not sure what's going on, but from the sound of it, I want to be included," Ballard said.

And so they left for the school. Carol couldn't say a word the whole way there. Her heart clogged her throat, and cold terror prickled her skin.

When they reached Loch Mallaig Elementary, Carol sprinted up the walk to the front door, paying no mind to the possibility of ice on the sidewalk. Once inside the first set of doors, it took all the restraint she had not to pound on the interior door, locked because school was in session. Instead, she jabbed the buzzer as the rest of the group gathered around her.

The wait for a reply felt endless, but Carol knew it could be measured in mere seconds. "Yes?" a voice crackled from the speaker.

"This is Carol MacCallan. Please, let me in."

"No problem. Good morning, Mrs. MacCallan." Carol heard the door latch disengage and hauled open the door so quickly that it nearly hit Harvey. He silently dodged it and followed her inside.

The group raced past the office. They'd nearly reached the end of the hall when they heard someone shouting from the office that they needed to sign in. If anyone responded, Carol didn't notice.

She was almost within touching distance of Kendra's classroom door when Harvey hauled her back. "Look first," he whispered. "Then burst in."

Everything in Carol wanted to pull away. Her daughter was in there. Her grandchildren could be. But she nodded and leaned carefully closer to see inside with Harvey beside her. A tiny whimper slipped from her before she could suppress it.

Through the small window in the door, she saw Byron. He was holding a gun. Both Doris and Camilla were facing him, but neither woman seemed the least bit afraid. Carol wasn't sure if that was good or incredibly bad. She repositioned herself slightly to see the rest of the room. No children were inside, and she almost whimpered again from relief. She didn't know where the twins could be, but she hoped desperately that they were safe.

Still, the absence of the children was comforting for only a moment. Carol spotted Jenny and Kendra, both bound to the short classroom chairs. Byron must have tied them up after Jenny answered her call. She felt Harvey ease away from her, but Carol couldn't move, couldn't tear her gaze from the scene before her, where one of her worst fears played out in real time.

Carol could hear Harvey whispering behind her, clearly explaining the situation to the others.

"We should wait for the police," Fergus said.

Carol faced them. "That man is extremely agitated, and it doesn't appear that Doris and Camilla are backing down. We can't wait. My daughter is in there."

"So what should we do?" Molly asked.

"I can talk him down," Ballard said. "I've known Byron all his life. I know that he respects me. I can help."

"And if not," Carol said, almost afraid to say what she thought, "I have another idea. While Ballard is distracting him, I can go through the other door and get the hostages out of there."

"You are not doing that alone," Harvey said.

"And you're not coming," Carol whispered. "You're too big and bulky. This has to be a stealth operation."

"I'll come," Molly said, much to Fergus's obvious dismay. "I'm small and stealthy."

Harvey started to say something, but Fergus put a hand on his arm. "Might as well give it up. This is what we signed on for, watching the women we love try to kill us with worry."

Carol drew herself up to her full height. "Jenny is in there. If you think I'm going to stand by and watch my daughter sit in danger for one more second—"

Harvey held up a hand. "All right, all right. But be careful. And you don't go in until Ballard has the man engaged."

Carol and Molly agreed without hesitation. They ducked below the window on the classroom door, then headed quietly down to the next door. Once there, they signaled their readiness to the group.

Ballard opened the door and stepped in. Instantly Carol heard Byron's raised voice, though she couldn't quite make out the words. She carefully peeked in the window. Ballard had his hands up and Byron's full attention was on him. The teacher's back was to Carol and Molly.

Carol opened the door slowly and silently, and the two women crept in, moving low and slow.

Jenny's expression was frantic when they reached her. "Get out of here!" she mouthed.

Carol ignored her and began picking at the knot in the rope that bound her daughter's hands. Years of knitting had made Carol an expert at undoing complex knots, and she soon had her daughter free. As she worked, she occasionally checked on Byron to be sure Ballard was keeping him engaged.

Which was why she saw Camilla pick up a large ceramic coffee mug from Kendra's desk and test the heft of it in her hand. Byron's fixation on Ballard had put his back to more than Jenny and Kendra. He'd also turned his back on the principal and Doris.

Carol shook her head at the principal, hoping the woman would see. They needed to leave, not fight an armed man. If Camilla saw her, she paid her no mind. Instead, she passed a desk stapler to Doris.

"Byron," Ballard said. "I've told you so many times that your dad would be proud of who you are. But you have to ask yourself, would he be proud of you today?"

"I don't know!" Byron said, almost yelling the answer. "Because I can't ask him. I never got to ask him a single thing, because of these two." He gestured toward Camilla and Doris, moving as he did so. He saw not only the two of them, but also Molly dragging Kendra toward the door with Carol and Jenny right behind them.

"Nobody leaves!" Byron shouted, raising the gun.

In that instant, several things happened. The door where the rest of the group had waited burst open and Harvey charged in with a roar. Ballard leaped at Byron, tackling him at the exact moment that a sturdy coffee mug hurled by a furious principal connected with Byron's head.

The teacher went down hard under Ballard's tackle. Harvey and Fergus quickly joined him in holding Byron down. Byron had dropped his gun, and Carol rushed to scoop it up, using her scarf to avoid disturbing any fingerprint evidence. Not that she imagined they would need much evidence with as many witnesses as the police would have available.

Byron writhed on the floor and growled things that shouldn't be said in an elementary school.

Camilla leaned over him and snapped, "Stop that at once!"

To the absolute shock of everyone in the room, he did. Then again, as she took in Camilla's outraged face, Carol was pretty sure she would have followed the principal's orders as well.

Then Doris marched over and gave the man a sound kick, making him yelp. "I'd give you a lot more than that if I could," she growled. "You bashed my best friend in the head with a dumpster lid and left her to die. If it was up to me, we'd take you outside and do the same to you. But I'm going to make sure Meg gets real justice."

Kendra put an arm around her mother. "We all are."

Byron glared back without speaking.

Carol was finally able to relax when she heard the sound of approaching sirens.

On Sunday after her guests were done with a hearty brunch, Carol settled down at her kitchen table with a cup of coffee and peered seriously at her best friends. "Are you sure you don't mind if I go on this fishing trip with Harvey? I know I've left you both holding down the fort too much lately."

"We don't mind," Laura said. "We didn't mind any of the times we've told you we don't mind."

"But I'm leaving you with all the work of the clothing drive," Carol said.

"Hardly," Molly said. "Aren't you the one who delivered the first load of donations to The Closet this morning? Besides, you've offered that gorgeous sweater that you knitted. No one can say you didn't do your part. So give yourself a break and go. The sooner the better."

Carol laughed. "Don't let Harvey hear you say that. I told him I hated to leave on such short notice in the first place, and now he wants to shorten it even more." Harvey had insisted it would do them good to have a few days alone before his old friends arrived. Carol thought he was right, but it was hard to shake off the guilt.

"It'll be good for you both," Laura said, echoing Harvey's words without knowing it.

"At least Byron confessed to everything," Carol said. "Of course, he'd already told Doris and Camilla in front of Kendra and Jenny, so keeping it from the police would have been a little pointless. When he spotted Meg lurking near our car that night, he tried to run her off. That's when she told him the truth about the prank, and he flew into a rage and bashed her with the dumpster lid when she tried to get away."

Molly shuddered. "It's all so horrible."

"It is," Carol said. "But I won't lie. I am relieved that I don't have to worry about the twins anymore."

"I can't believe the man came to your house," Molly said with a shudder. "It sounds like he was actually thinking of harming you."

"He might have if Harvey hadn't scared him away," Carol said. "At least that's what he told the police. Apparently he was very chatty."

"I'm glad we're all safe," Laura said. "The note on the hearse was scary."

Molly gaped at her friend. "You didn't look scared."

"I take great care to never look scared," Laura said, then lifted her coffee mug for a sip.

Jenny leaned around one of the thick wooden posts that served as part of the boundary between the kitchen and the rest of the large open-plan front room. "You will not believe what I saw in your bedroom," she told her mother.

All eyes focused on her.

"What?" Carol asked.

"Maisie is on your bed reading to Pascal. And he's sitting beside her."

"Pascal?" Carol said. "He usually acts as if the twins want to eat him."

"I know," Jenny said. "He's not in her lap or letting her pet him, but this is major movement on the friendship scale."

"That's the magic of Maisie," Carol said. "That child never gives up."

"How are Kendra and Doris doing?" Laura asked.

Jenny slid into a chair at the table. "Doris has moved in with Kendra until she can get on her feet. Kendra said her grandparents are planning to come up today and maybe start some reconciliation. Everyone is going to be a little wary with each other at first, and they have a lot of hurt to work through, but I believe they'll find their way."

"I agree," Carol said. "They're all good people, and good people can do amazing things."

Jenny laughed. "As you prove constantly. I'm not always thrilled with the stuff you three get in to, but I'm going to try to have more faith."

"Don't have too much," Molly said. "We all need a little supervision to keep us in line."

They were chuckling when Maisie skipped into the room.

"I thought you were reading to Pascal," Carol said.

"I tried to pet him when I finished the book," Maisie said. "He's under the bed again."

"Still, you're making progress," her mother said. "Never give up."

"I won't," Maisie assured her. "I'm stubborn as a mule with twice the kick, same as you and Grandma!"

After the burst of laughter, Carol asked her where she'd heard that, though she suspected she knew.

"Grandpa," Maisie confirmed.

"Did I hear my name?" Harvey asked as he came through the door carrying an egg basket with Gavin and Craig following behind.

"Only spoken of fondly," Carol said. "Though we may talk later."

"I hope so." Harvey handed the basket to Jenny. "I walked Gavin and Craig through their chicken duties for when we're gone. Turns out, the hens were feeling generous today and I have two eggs you can take home."

"But I don't want any," Gavin said.

"Why?" Jenny asked.

"Gavin got to see one of the hens lay an egg right in front of him," Harvey said.

"Didn't you know where eggs come from, Gavin?" Craig asked.

Gavin put his hands on his hips and spoke in world-weary tone. "I know, but it's different when you see it with your own two eyes. Something like that—it changes a guy."

And as the adults fought the giggles, Harvey clapped his grandson on the back. "I couldn't have said it better myself."

Carol sat back for a moment and savored the scene before her—beloved friends and family gathered together, enjoying each other's company. As a smile played on her lips, she thought to herself that life simply didn't get any better than this. She was truly blessed.

Up to this point, we've been doing all the writing. Now it's *your* turn!

Tell us what you think about this book, the characters, the bad guy, or anything else you'd like to share with us about this series. We can't wait to hear from *you*!

Log on to give us your feedback at:
https://www.surveymonkey.com/r/ScottishBakehouse

Annie's FICTION